SHOWDOWN

A DESCENTVERSE NOVEL

S M REINE

CONTENTS

My earliest writing was fanfic, before I knew fanfic was a thing. In the dark ages before the internet became what it is now, I wrote stories about the X-Men, Sailor Moon, and Animorphs on an IBM Compatible, which firmly dates me as a 90s kid.

I transitioned into publishing fiction online as soon as I "discovered" it. You could find me on early Buffy the Vampire Slayer websites, writing fanfic about Faith, then Illyria and Wesley. Bigger sites began to emerge, and I sharpened my teeth with Harry Potter on Fanfiction.net.

The serialized format of fanfic is intensely appealing to me. I love writing shorter amounts of fiction—a chapter, or maybe just a scene—and posting it more frequently so that I get reader feedback on every bit. I love to adjust the story to reader comments.

I lost time for fanfic when I began self-publishing novels, because at first, I published books so quickly it was nearly the same thing. I published a book every month or so for years. This built into an urban fantasy world I call the Descentverse, for my first popular series. I'm proud of this body of work. It was exhilarating to produce in such a rush—and exhausting.

A decade into my career, with children and other hobbies (gasp), I no longer have the time or stamina to publish in quantity that quickly.

Still, I miss getting to be involved with my readers while writing stories. That's where Showdown came from: A serialized web story featuring battles between my characters, where readers got to choose the winner of each fight.

The Descentverse Showdown was a delightful few weeks where I got to revisit older characters, pit unusual powers against each other, and talk with my readers. A lot.

In a sense, this story is fanfiction I've written for my own universe. It's not canonical. It's largely metatextual, reflecting on the role the Descentverse has played in my life. And it was written in a way that involved readers directly, actively, one chapter at a time.

Because this story was written on-the-fly, it might feel a bit more slapdash than the other books. The erratic path a serialized, interactive story takes is part of the charm. Fanfic is pure passion.

I've edited Showdown to clean up most of the typos and smooth out the language, but the actual plot remains the way I wrote it, without structural changes, in order to respect the experience.

You probably won't get a lot out of this book if you're not a hardcore Descentverse fan. There are spoilers for all my books in these pages. I'd recommend closing this and starting with one of my many free books, which you can find on my website: http://smreine.com/

Otherwise: I wrote Showdown for *you*. the one who has printed out the reading list on my website, checked off all the boxes, and went back to print a new reading list and start over. You know my books better than I do. You're kind of amazing.

Some readers had a shocked or worried reaction to the depiction of the Army of Evil in this story. They are sadistic, truly evil. Flora and Louise are the cruel emcees here, but in reality, truly wonderful kind people who moderate my fan group.

To be clear, I don't perceive my readers as cruel, sadistic, or evil—quite the opposite. I've been blessed with a readership that overflows with love and compassion. But the greatest compliment I pay to people I love is turning them into villains. Villains are my favorite. I don't care about Batman, but Harley and Ivy live in my soul. Ann Friedman is lovingly based upon my best friend. I hope that you can see how the sadism means I love y'all too, haha.

Thanks for playing in this world with me. Thanks for wading into this darkness. We're here together.

—Sara, February 2020

SHOWDOWN

1

NOVEMBER 9, 2019.

Rylie Gresham woke at three o'clock in the morning, and she wasn't certain why. Her bedroom was still and her werewolf ears could tell the world outside was asleep. The sanctuary had been peaceful as of late; with the new hospital facilities, freshly built downtown, and the new Academy under construction, everyone was kept productively busy. Too busy to fight. Too busy to stay awake at night when the air hung with a quiet chill.

Her mate, Abel, wasn't with her. *Is something wrong?*

She donned her bathrobe and padded to the kids' room. Benjamin slept peacefully, sprawled over the toddler bed he refused to trade for a Big Boy Bed. His baby sister slept peacefully on a floor mat because she kept climbing out of the crib. Rylie's aunt, Gwyneth, took the twin bed, and the zombie would have woken if they needed anything. They hadn't roused Rylie.

"Then why am I awake?" Rylie whispered to herself, shutting their door silently.

And where is Abel?

She headed barefoot into the night. It wasn't too cold for a werewolf Alpha. Her breath came out as fog while her toes scrunched against ice. The clouds had vanished. It felt like the stars were watching her.

A wind lifted. It smelled of coffee, whiskey, and cannabis. Rylie's nose wrinkled at the scent, turning to look for the source—

—and she found herself facing a stadium.

It was an open dirt was lit by fires around the edges. Across that pit, the benches were filled with a quiet group, watching the ground with anticipation. Rylie's acute eyes could make out every detail of the onlookers in the darkness. Her nose told her that if she was in some kind of strange viewing box, there were others next to hers, occupied by other people.

The entire world had changed in a blink and she'd felt no sense of movement.

Shock rolled through Rylie's body. She tried to take a quick step back onto her stairs, but they weren't there. She bumped a stone bench hard enough to bruise her ankle.

"Ow!"

"Careful," said a lovely young woman with mounds of chestnut curls, who sat against the wall in the corner.

She looked familiar. Her luminous white-blue eyes were the signature mark of an angel, which put Rylie's hackles on edge. She'd met few angels who she could trust. "Who are you? Where am I?" Rylie asked.

"I'm Marion," said the girl.

Rylie blinked. "No you're not." Marion was one of Ariane Garin's daughters, and she was an adorable schoolchild with too much attitude and little respect for adults. She'd spent last summer staying with Rylie. She wasn't even tall as Rylie's ribcage yet, much less a gazelle-legged supermodel with glowing eyes, a designer gown, and eerily calm features.

"You look young, which explains why you don't know me like this," Marion said thoughtfully. "I don't think you and I were pulled from the same year. Where did you wake up today?"

"The sanctuary," Rylie said. "Um, in 2019."

"Ah, yes. It's 2032 for me." Marion hugged herself, even though the stadium was warm. She shivered. "Don't try to leave. We can't. Whoever brought us here—"

The fires blazed higher, erupting with a boom that washed charcoal heat over Rylie. The crowd erupted with cheers, launching from their benches to wave their arms over their heads. They were a diverse crew, from what Rylie could see and smell. There were demons, sidhe, angels, and humans among them, mingled as one.

Something was beginning.

Rylie edged to the waist-high wall overlooking the stadium. A pair of people walked into the dirt pit.

"Army of Evil, we hear you!" roared a beast of a woman with a cat coiled around her shoulders. She wore all leather. She was plastered in so many tattoos that hardly a bare inch showed. "You want a showdown of heroes? We'll give you a showdown of heroes!"

"Showdown?" Rylie echoed in a whisper.

"I'm Louise the Monster," went on the woman. "This here's Flora the Destroya. Make some noise!"

They lifted their arms to receive the adulation. Rylie clutched her heart, adrenaline rising at the sound.

Flora had sharp eyes and a mischievous smile. "We've pulled twenty champions from every world we could reach—the infernal and ethereal planes, and the Middle Worlds—at the times when these heroes were strongest. All of them veterans of war. And none of them have any choice but to fight for our entertainment!"

This pleased the crowd too—this Army of Evil.

Rylie grabbed the half-wall so she could lean out and look for somewhere to escape. But she butted against an invisible wall. It zinged like she'd made the mistake of blow drying her hair with wet hands again. She jerked back.

"Fights are to the death," said Flora. "Two by two, we're going to narrow these heroes down to person standing!"

"They won't be dead forever," added Louise. "Once they drop dead, they're going back to their lives with no memory of this. There are no costs. No consequences. Just glorious battle! And today, we're starting with two of the greatest—Elise Kavanagh, from the Breaking, and Deirdre Tombs from the first election for Alpha werewolf!"

Iron gates rolled open from either end of the pit. Rylie's heart splashed into her stomach as she watched the two woman enter.

Elise Kavanagh was a demon. Pale flesh, flowing black hair, and looking pissed as hell. Rylie pitied her opponent until she saw an unfamiliar shifter stroll into the arena...and immediately catch fire, standing in the midst of a blazing inferno. Rylie had never heard of a shapeshifter who could catch fire. This was something else entirely.

"Who's ready for some fun?" shouted Flora.

2

After they made their introductions, Flora and Louise cleared the stadium so swiftly that Seth didn't see them leave. They were simply gone, leaving nothing in the arena except for Elise and her enemy.

Seth watched with grim resignation—the same expression he saw on James Faulkner's face at his side.

"Elise is going to be fine," Seth said.

"I know," James said, but it didn't seem to assuage his concern.

He had reason to fear. Seth now understood the rules of this game, which would pit survivor against survivor until none were left. If Elise won this battle, there would be more to come. Eventually, either Seth or James would likely face her.

That was when the real trouble would start.

Seth wasn't sure who he would bet on. He studied the man who shared his cell, trying to decide what era James Faulkner was considered at the peak of his power. At this point, James Faulkner had white hair and bright-blue eyes. His skin was tattooed with magical runes. He was hard-jawed, tense in the shoulders, pulled somehow from the midst of some distant battle to this place.

This man could easily be Seth's death.

There was no period of time where Seth could win against James. At his weakest, he was still the most powerful witch in the world; at his strongest, he was the God of Life who held Time's heart.

On the other hand, Seth knew exactly where he had come from. He had woken that morning in the year 2035, and gone to bed with his wife, Marion. He was an avatar of the God of Death—barely a shadow of the form he held in the Infinite. Seth could have matched a werewolf. Another god would easily crush him.

And if James didn't destroy him, it would be one of the women in the arena now.

Deirdre Tombs flared with fire that rippled over her skin. She gritted her teeth, balled her fists, and faced the Godslayer. Seth remembered seeing her on the news when Rylie first held a democratic election for Alpha. Deirdre Tombs had been part of a radical splinter group of shifters—a murderer. A terrorist.

"I don't like this," Deirdre said. Her voice echoed clearly over the crackling of her flames. They were brighter than the fires circling the fighting ring.

"I don't like it either." Elise spread her arms and her hair rippled into darkness. She was ready to fight. Resigned to face this enemy.

The Army hadn't stopped roaring for them to fight, and there was no way out of this stadium. James had already tried to escape. If he couldn't make it out, nobody could.

And Deirdre wasn't going to back down.

Elise shattered into a thousand fragments of darkness and dived for Deirdre. Seth had seen her swallow people whole like that. He expected Deirdre to vanish instantly.

But the terrorist shapeshifted as quickly. Deirdre shed her human skin for a firebird so big that the blaze blinded Seth and sent heat rippling over his skin, even from the cell he shared with James. When she opened her mouth in a cry, the sound that came out was the shriek of an ancient bird, echoing through the stands.

Elise's shadow crashed against Deirdre's light.

Energy boomed. Dust shook free from the roof, peppering Seth's shoulders. He gripped the wall to stay standing.

When the explosion faded, nothing remained but darkness.

The shadow collapsed on itself, retracting, shrinking, shriveling. A white-skinned form appeared at its heart. Elise Kavanagh swayed on her feet, hands pressed against her belly, pain on her face.

She burped. A flaming feather and ash puffed from her mouth.

The Army screamed.

"Elise Kavanagh has killed Deirdre Tombs!" said Louise, her voice magically amplified. She had taken an emcee's box on the opposite end of the stadium.

"Who wants the next one?" Flora asked.

The crowd hadn't even calmed down yet, so they frothed harder at the baiting, and Seth was sick at the sound of it.

There was no waiting, no more time.

"Coming up next..."

The world bowed around Seth. His cell vanished. He found himself standing outside one of those huge iron gates on the same level as the fighting ring, and he realized he was next.

James waited behind the other door. His pale, rune-marked skin glowed with magic and reflected the fire.

"Shit," Seth muttered.

He gripped the door and pressed his face against

the bars, looking up into the crowd. There were several boxes where competitors were held. He could make out his wife watching—she was easy to spot with those glowing eyes. And she stood beside Rylie.

"*Shit*," he said again, with all the passion he could muster.

The gate jerked in his hands. It lifted.

Seth emerged into the arena and reached reflexively into his jacket. There was a gun. He was surprised. At least he had his Beretta.

"And now for a battle of the gods!" said Louise's growling voice. "James Faulkner, destined to become the God of Life, a mage who innovated paper magic!"

"And Seth Wilder, an avatar of the God of Death! Fight!"

3

Marion Garin had never been one to shy away from a fight, nor was she the type to fear for her husband's life. It wasn't necessary. They had been fighting infernal incursions along the Pacific coast for years, and Seth had a way of surviving the most dire scraps. It had nothing to do with the fact he was also the God of Death. In this form, as an avatar, he was little stronger than a normal man. But he was brilliant, quick, clever—a survivor.

It was one of the things she loved most about him.

The sight of Seth approaching James, of all people, to meet at the heart of the stadium made Marion sick.

"No, no, no," she whispered, digging her finger-nails into the half-wall.

James had taught Marion most of the magic she knew. He was as ruthless as Seth was compassionate.

If there was anyone who could kill the man she loved, it was James.

"I'm not going to fight," Seth said, loudly enough for his voice to echo over the screaming army.

He reached out, dropped his gun.

"We thought someone was likely to pull that," Flora said, sounding amused rather than concerned. "But we can't have any of you backing out, can we? That's not *fun*. And our Army of Evil *loves* to have fun!"

"If he won't fight, I won't hurt him," James declared. His voice was hoarse, as if he'd been screaming and lost the ability to speak.

The army booed. They shook their fists. Words formed from the noise: *Fight. Cowards. Do it.*

"Don't worry, don't worry." Louise scratched her kitty's chin, smirking. "We have a few options to keep things moving, and most of them are more dignified than cattle prods. But none of them are pretty." She snapped her fingers.

A light flooded Marion and Rylie's cell, illumi-nating them.

Seth's eyes connected with Marion's.

She had loved him from the first moment they

saw each other. Neither of them had known themselves at the time. Marion's memory had been stolen by the gods, and Seth had been oblivious to his soul's ascendance. But something inside of her had instantly known something inside of him. That connection remained now, and it was as thrilling as the first time, no matter how many thousands of times they had shared a bed.

Marion shook her head. Even if Flora and Louise intended to torture her to death, it changed nothing. Seth shouldn't fight. "Don't," she mouthed.

"Do you want to do this the easy way or the hard way?" Flora asked, drawing a fireball from inside her jacket. It danced over her fingertips. She confided to Louise in a stage whisper, "I've always wanted to say that."

She pulled back as if to hurl the flame at Marion.

Seth picked up his gun again.

"*Don't*," Marion said again. "It's what they want."

"You know he won't let them hurt anyone." Rylie glanced between them. "But why…? How?"

This younger Rylie wouldn't know of Seth and Marion's wedding. The Alpha may have been young enough that she only knew Marion as a child, which would make the marriage confusing—even repulsive.

Marion couldn't bring herself to explain. The

only words she could find were, "We have no time to discuss the intricacies of time."

With Seth arming himself, James was moving too. "Truly, you are the foulest of foul," James snarled at the announcers.

"Thank you," said Flora.

James stripped his shirt off. His physique was lean, as if starved down to the minimum of ropey muscle, and every inch was patterned in runes. Magic sizzled over his hands. It had that acidic pre-Genesis tang to it, which Marion only encountered in artifacts. This was an older, more primal version of James.

But this was just Seth—her Seth, a reluctant avatar who never wanted to see another man die.

Seth lifted his gun.

James shot first.

He pointed a finger, his mouth opened, and the entire stadium shook. The wave that hit Seth would be invisible to most. Marion was an angel. She could see every excruciating moment of James's clumsy magecraft unfolding, blossoming in runes both beautiful and devastating.

Marion could cast no magic to counter it. Not through the wards on her cell.

She could do nothing but watch her master destroy her beloved.

Seth took it in the chest. He flew into the wall

and cracked the stones, slamming to the ground.

Marion's heart leaped into her throat. She thought he was already dead.

Seth came up underneath a second wave tossed by James. He shot blindly—honestly, a skill he'd perfected—and silver-tinged crimson splattered from James's shoulder.

James snarled and slapped a hand over the wound. A tattoo flared on his wrist with the scent of ozone. When his fingers dropped, the wound was closed—and he was hurling another spell.

Seth darted away, dodging again, and the next one. Then instead of trying to shoot James again, he leaped for the wall under Marion and Rylie's cell.

Rage surged through Marion, and she punched her hand through the wards holding the cell. It burned her arm. The skin writhed on her bones.

"Seth!" Marion threw a hand down to catch his. Their fingers brushed.

An image flashed through her mind: Deirdre Tombs, lying in a dark room. Not dead. Not gone back to her own time. But in some kind of cell.

Is she still alive?

Flame arced from the ceiling. Marion only had a heartbeat to wonder what was hurling fireballs before it hit her—right in the chest.

Seth's hand slipped away. She tumbled into

Rylie's arms, crying out at the searing pain. She slapped at her flesh.

Her dress was smoldering, and the skin underneath felt cold, and she was going to burn to death. And none of that felt as terrible as what she knew was happening to Seth while she writhed on the floor.

Marion summoned the right spell after too long—once she'd already lost half her bodice and the skin underneath looked like brisket. Another spell served as salve for the pain. To stop the burning. To start regrowing her skin.

But by the time she dragged herself to her knees, it was too late. Her dress was shredded, and Seth was gone.

Louise the Monster's voice bounced around the arena.

"James Faulkner kills Seth Wilder by stopping his heart with electricity," she said.

The audience was still so damn delighted.

"We can't fight," Rylie said through gritted teeth. Her fingertips were bleeding. She'd lost her fingernails. Fangs flashed through her lips when she spoke. "What can they do to us? Hurt someone we care about? We're all going to get hurt anyway. We're going to *die*. We can't fight!"

Marion said, "I don't know if it matters."

Before the last word came out, the world lurched around her.

She reappeared on the other side of an iron grate, looking into the arena as Seth's body was dragged away and James limped toward Marion's door. He collapsed against the inner wall when he got there. Not so much a victor so much as a survivor. The runes he'd activated left welts on his skin.

He turned apologetic eyes on Marion, but he didn't look nearly contrite enough. He didn't know he had just destroyed Marion's world. He didn't know how much she was hurting. Most likely, this version of James didn't recognize her, just as Rylie hadn't.

Marion swallowed down her anger. "Find Deirdre," she hissed, gripping his arm.

The gate opened again. It was time for Marion to step out.

"Our next battle features the retired Voice of God, former Steward of the Winter Court, sister to the Godslayer, bride of Death—Marion Wilder! A master mage with style to spare!"

She felt none of her usual stylishness staggering into the pen. That's all it was—a pen where they waited to be butchered.

Rylie emerged from the other side.

"Marion *Wilder*?" she asked.

Many of Marion's friends hadn't taken their

husband's name after marriage. It was less common day by day, as the survivors of Genesis clung to their bloodlines. But she had no attachment to her mother's surname. She didn't want her father's. And she had never loved as she loved Seth.

Marion always suspected that Rylie felt the same for Seth.

Rylie and Seth were high school sweethearts, so to speak. They had been in love with the dire urgency of teenagers. But Rylie had cheated on him, left him for his brother. Abel Wilder was also an Alpha werewolf. A better match.

What the beast wanted wasn't what the woman wanted. Marion could see that the desperation lived on, deep in her golden eyes. She had learned that Seth married another at the same time she watched him die.

Rylie Gresham was breaking.

Her bones were already popping, her dress fallen away. She was shapeshifting. Her golden eyes were glowing. She was ready for some kind of fight—and Marion couldn't be certain Rylie wouldn't kill her to protect someone else.

She had to be ready.

"The second fighter is Rylie Gresham, the First Alpha! She may not look like much, but just wait until she goes full furry," said Flora the Destroya.

"We've seen this girl take down demons the size of skyscrapers. Haven't we, Louise?"

Rylie's slavering jaws extended into a muzzle. The humanity drained from her eyes. There was nothing but grief and the blank violence of a caged animal—someone who now felt fiercely jealous of Marion Wilder.

And there was nothing left to do but fight.

4

Everton Stark stood in a cage within a cage. Unlike most competitors, he hadn't been left free to move; he was trapped in silver shackles, just like his cellmate.

Abel Wilder was watching Rylie Gresham fight eagerly, also just like Stark. But they had wildly different reasons for being riveted by the battle. Abel surely prayed that his mate would emerge alive.

Stark, on the other hand, was only hoping to see a miserable werewolf Alpha die.

"C'mon, Rylie," Abel muttered, his voice a low growl.

For all there was to say about Rylie, she was an Alpha to her core. When she saw Marion's hands leap with magic, it took bare moments for her to shapeshift, flaying her own skin to reveal the wolf within. She was enormous but sleek. A wolf blown by the wind with her fur like rays of sunlight. Stark had felt the bite of those teeth and lived to tell of it, but only because his monster within was even more monstrous.

He could take her, he was certain. He had done it before.

"C'mon, c'mon," Abel said. "Don't hurt anyone, Rylie..."

Stark realized with a jolt that Abel was urging his mate *not* to hurt Marion. How could he be on the team of another woman?

"Vile," Stark said in a deep growl. "Wishing for your mate to lose."

"Rylie won't ever forgive herself if she kills another person like this," Abel snapped. "She almost didn't make it last time. When the wolf takes over, she gets suicidal. All right?"

Then Stark's assumption was wrong. Either way, it was laughable.

"She'll survive if she's sane," Stark said. "Survival is the only choice."

"That's delusional! Our captors are never going to let us out of here," snarled the other man. "We're all gonna die against Elise. Did you see her eat a phoenix?"

Stark had seen it, and he had known a strange kind of longing at Deirdre's death. He had seen her die before. It never got easier. Yet he believed she would survive, even if nobody else did, even if their hosts were lying about the terms of the game. Deirdre was hard to kill. Sometimes that infuriated him. Today, it pleased him.

Rylie flashed toward Marion with the breathtaking speed of a werewolf. The beast had taken charge.

Marion took the defensive, lifting her arms to cast shields of magic. She deflected the first snap of Rylie's jaw with a spray of sparks. She leaped and rolled away from the second bite, but didn't seem especially agile; her scorched dress was caught in the wolf's teeth.

The werewolf snapped her head and sent Marion flying.

Angel wings flared behind her, spreading to catch herself. She slowed her spin through the air. But still, Marion struck the wall, and it was hard enough to daze her.

"Seth showed me a vision, Rylie," Marion said quietly. Stark could only hear her because she'd fallen near his cage. The werewolf's sensitive ears would be able to hear Marion as well from the opposite end of the arena. "Something strange happened to the first loser. She didn't die. We have to figure out—"

She broke off with a scream.

Rylie had moved so fast even Stark couldn't see it. One swipe of a paw was all it took.

Gashes opened on Marion's belly. She bled as she fell, crying out.

A mage of her ability likely could have bound the wounds, healing herself quickly. But she would have to get away from Rylie to do that. The Alpha was a wild animal and Marion had stumbled into her forest. Rylie bit down, shook her head, and tossed.

The angel hit the ground a rag doll a few meters away.

"Rylie Gresham wins!" called Flora.

The Army of Evil cheered. They were ready for the next fight.

Stark had already decided to survive.

It didn't matter if the fight was rigged. For the last several months, Stark had been imprisoned by the Office of Preternatural Affairs. They hadn't taken kindly to his killing spree while hunting for Rylie Gresham's office as Alpha. He had been muzzled like an animal.

This Army of Evil was giving him a chance to fight Abel Wilder, a loathsome sanctuary werewolf.

It was an upgrade, and he was happy to play the game.

The cage vanished from around Stark. He was transported instantly to the gateway from whence Marion had emerged, no longer trapped within bars.

Stark growled his satisfaction. He rolled out the muscles of his broad shoulders and clenched his fists.

"The next fight is a perfect match," said Louise the Monster. "Abel Wilder's the Alpha mate of the sanctuary—an experienced hunter and powerful werewolf who leads thousands of his kind. He's facing down with Everton Stark, a Brotherhood Ard, and one of the rarest shifters we've ever seen. Not quite wolf, not quite bear, and so hard to defeat that even Rylie's lost to him before!"

The gate rolled up on them, and there was nothing between Stark and Abel.

Abel's face showed no reluctance. Neither of them would hold back.

Simultaneously, they began to shift.

"Fight!"

5

Fritz Friederling wasn't having a good time. There should have been *something* fun about watching the various thorns in the Office of Preternatural Affairs's paws killing each other one by one, but it was difficult to enjoy himself when death appeared imminent.

He had been pulled from his desk at work for this. Death was slightly preferable to working under Lucrezia de Angelis's stiletto, assuming death weren't too onerous, too jealous, or too blond, like his organization's vice president.

So far, Fritz was optimistic. His waiting opponent was an attractive thirty-something kopis with a pencil mustache. He didn't ping Fritz's senses as a kopis, or any other kind of preternatural, so he was probably just a demon hunter.

"Hey, I'm Anthony Morales. I guess it's some kind of honor to meet you." He offered a hand to Fritz to shake. He managed to grin, even though he was drenched in a nervous sweat. He seemed to recognize Fritz. "Twenty on the big guy."

The "big guy," Everton Stark, had shapeshifted into a bear-wolf, according to the emcees in charge, and he was big indeed. Fritz was glad he hadn't gotten pitted against the man. He may have been a kopis imbued with super-strength, but that was his only preternatural gift. His other powers were institutional, from banks and government offices, which could not reach here to save him.

Abel Wilder turned into a black wolf that nearly matched Stark in size. Blood and other fluids sprayed in a wide diameter around him. His roar made the stone walls of Fritz's cell shake.

"My money's on Wilder," Fritz said. "I've followed his story. He's impressive." There was an inch-thick file at the bottom of his filing cabinet on the man. Abel had only recently risen as Alpha of America's remaining werewolves. Before that, he'd been a deadly hunter, with a dozen kills credited to his name. His mother had worked for the OPA, so Fritz had been hoping to employ him until the bite.

"I know who he is," Anthony said. "But like, that's *Everton Stark*. He singlehandedly threatened the whole sanctuary power structure. Dude's smart and strong."

"What sanctuary?" Fritz asked.

Anthony frowned. "Aren't you Secretary Friederling?"

"The title is director," he said. "Secretary of what, exactly?"

Stark showed his strength by slamming into Abel. They rolled into a snarling mass of fur and claws, and their violence seemed to delight the army. This was the kind of battle they'd wanted to see: two vicious opponents out for blood, with none of the emotional complexity weighing on the likes of Marion.

"I guess you're not from my part of the timeline," Anthony said. "Everything I know about time travel comes from Doctor Who, so I think I'm not supposed to give you spoilers about the future."

"Fair enough," Fritz said. He doubted either of them would live long enough for spoilers to matter, though.

At least the Friederling line wouldn't end in a boring way. Secretary of anything sounded dull.

Stark ripped open Abel's flank. Fresh blood splattered the arena and sizzled against fire.

He didn't slow. If anything, the injury made him faster. The black wolf was a blur darting around the arena, dogging Stark's rear to snap where the bear-wolf wasn't agile enough to retaliate.

"I don't think we should fight," Anthony said. "When it's our turn, let's try something else. Let's go after the announcers."

An intriguing idea. "They must have some kind of protection against that," Fritz said.

Stark's roar shattered the air.

Abel's teeth had sunken into his throat. He shredded it, sending fur and blood spraying. "Oof," Anthony said.

"Still betting on the big guy?" Fritz asked.

Stark swung around to pin Abel. He was fast enough to succeed—and fast enough to pin him with the top of his body, leaving his back paws free to rake deep wounds down Abel's haunches.

"Yeah," Anthony said. "But seriously, we oughta go after the biggest guys here. And those are the ones with the microphone."

"I think they're using magical amplification, actually," Fritz said.

Abel hurled Stark into the wall below Fritz's cell. The floor shook. The fires around the arena flamed higher and the audience cheered. They were shouting Abel's name. They had chosen their champion.

These people wanted to see Stark die.

Fritz took another look at Anthony—his

appealing features, his jaded smirk, his terrible mustache. He would be a fan favorite. They'd call for Fritz's death next.

"Yes," he said, "let's go after the ones in charge."

Stark died when Abel's mouth closed around his skull. The black wolf crushed the top of Stark's head into hamburger. Fritz idly considered the fact that if he died in battle, his last meal would have been the leftover tamales Agent Hawke brought in that morning.

Stark vanished, leaving Abel's fur drenched. He shook himself off. Fritz was sprayed from his vantage point.

"Ugh," he said, wiping a sleeve over his eyes. "Disgusting."

The complaint fell on an empty room.

He'd vanished from his cell, reappearing at the level of the arena. Anthony was no longer with Fritz.

The iron grate rose. Abel had returned to his naked human form by the time he stumbled through the gate, gasping. Stark had wounded him deeply. Even an Alpha werewolf was struggling to heal the gaps torn wide in his flesh, exposing glistening meat within.

Fritz would have died within moments. Abel would be fine, eventually.

"Kill those bastards," Abel snarled at Fritz, as if they knew each other.

Fritz adjusted his cufflinks, as if they were any kind of armor to protect him from what would come. "I'll see what I can do."

He met Anthony in the center of the arena. It was more difficult to see the Army of Evil from that perspective. He could only make out Flora and Louise in their box above it all. They looked entirely too comfortable.

Fritz's hand slipped into his jacket. He had a gun where he always carried one.

Anthony was now armed too, a shotgun mounted on his spine.

It could be a fast battle. An ugly battle.

Or it didn't have to be a battle at all.

"This fight pits the Director of the Magical Violations Department, Fritz Friederling, against founding member of the Hunting Club, Anthony Morales. One is a pre-Genesis kopis, and the other used to be. Rarer than a pink elephant in a zoo!" said Louise, laughing at her own comparison. Flora giggled with her. The mood was still so light. The Army was delighted to see the men squaring off as if about to box in a match.

There was no winning this.

"Fight!" Flora said.

So Fritz drew his gun, swung it high, and fired a shot off at the emcees.

Pain exploded in his arm. He clapped a hand over

a wound that appeared from nowhere—no, from his bullet ricocheting off a magical shield protecting the announcers.

Of course they were protected.

"I told you guys to fight," Flora said, sounding unbothered by this.

A spotlight fell on another cell, illuminating a buxom blond woman within. Fritz didn't recognize her. If she was in the OPA's files, then she wasn't someone significant enough to catch his attention.

But Anthony recognized her. His breath caught in his throat, and he made a sound very much like choking.

"Betty?"

"Fight," Flora said again, reminding them why they were there, what they could do.

"Hollow threats won't force us to do anything," Fritz tried to say. "Throw fireballs at everyone here. We aren't going to fight."

Then he heard the whisper of metal against leather, and he turned to see Anthony drawing the shotgun from his leather sheath. Whoever the blond woman was—relative, girlfriend, cohort—her presence was enough to change Anthony's tune.

Behind him, another cell had been illuminated. Agent Hawke had been taken too. The big oaf was shaking his fists at the air. "Shoot 'em again, Friederling!" Was that supposed to make Fritz want to protect him? Cèsar was only an employee. They couldn't know how closely Fritz had been watching him.

Lightning arced from the roof. It blasted Cèsar, and he vanished behind the half-wall of his cell. Fritz nearly swallowed his own tongue.

"No," he said.

One of the emcees said again: "Fight!"

And the Army chanted along: *Fight. Fight. Fight.*

Fritz lifted his gun. Anthony pumped his shotgun. Their eyes met.

Silently, simultaneously, they came to an agreement and nodded.

6

Cèsar was a weird mix of heartsick and happy, watching Fritz facing Anthony in the arena. Cèsar liked both of them. But he loved Fritz. And this was Fritz in his prime, as a kopis, not the tired old man that Cèsar had been married to for thirty years.

Before the abduction, Cèsar had been safe and comfortable in Haven with his partners. He had been arguing with Fritz over which of them got to eat the last of Isobel's cookies. He'd made an ice skating rink using his powers as cait sidhe, one of the strongest survivors of Ofelia's Winter Court, and watched neighborhood kids having fun.

And now this.

Wrenched away from his ice skating rink, his cookie, and his tired old man.

He loved his tired old man, maybe even more than he'd loved Fritz before. But this younger version of Fritz reminded him of their daughter. She had that strong-backed, confident stride, paired with a sort of insolent cast to her mouth. He was feisty, fiery, a survivor.

Fritz might stand a chance. The idea of him losing hurt too much to consider.

"If the bad guys are going to kidnap us from different timelines, why can't we just sit down for a tea party?" Cèsar asked his cellmate. "We could entertain them with jokes."

Shatter Cage was running his hands over the back wall of the cell. He'd identified himself as a phoenix, like Deirdre Tombs, and fire licked along his knuckles as he searched. "Sentimentality later. Escaping now."

"It's just, Fritz has both of his legs," Cèsar said. "I bet he can still hear in his left ear. I wanna hang out with him. I don't want him dying, or *me* dying..."

Oh great, and now Anthony and Fritz were exchanging gunfire. That was terrible for Cèsar's nerves.

Fritz looked hot when he dodged gunfire, though.

"Here it is," Cage said.

He shoved a blast of flame through a crack in the wall.

Cèsar stood to get a better view. The phoenix had not only discovered a crack in the protections, but widened it enough to squeeze fingers inside.

"How'd you do that?"

"It's a combination of the Blessing of Silverclaw and the Messenger's Gift, obviously," Cage said, as if this were some term Cèsar should have known. Cage came from the future. He'd been vague about the year, just like he'd been vague about his powers as phoenix, and vague about his plan once they escaped that cell. "No wards can hold me. Not even meta-wards."

"Meta-wards?" Cèsar asked.

"The only problem is that I can't shatter this crack," Cage said. "VexEn got disconnected by the temporal elements of this abduction, so that's no use, and I can't download charms to blast this apart!"

"I literally have no idea what you're saying."

There was one more gunshot, and then the crowd roared.

Cèsar almost didn't want to look.

He couldn't resist.

Fritz was on the ground, facedown, with Anthony standing over him. It looked like Anthony had plugged a shotgun shell straight into Fritz's jacket. The sight of it made sidhe power shimmer over Cèsar's skin as angry defensiveness filled him.

But then Anthony stepped over to nudge Fritz with a toe...

And there was one more, smaller gunshot. Not from a shotgun, but from the handgun Fritz had palmed, shooting up under his arm. The aim must have been lucky. He went under Anthony's chin and took off the top of his head.

Another perfectly nice person died, bleeding, on the stone.

"Fuck," Cèsar muttered.

He should have been eating that cookie right now.

"You said you're cait sidhe, right?" Cage asked from the rear of the cell. "Your magic might be able to blow this. It's our turn to fight next, so hurry. Just stick a finger in the crack and let out the cat."

Cèsar was rooted to the spot, holding his breath while waiting to see if the younger version of his husband would survive.

Fritz got onto his knees and shed his jacket, revealing standard OPA body armor. He was bruised, bloody, and panting...but alive. For now.

"Fritz Friederling plays possum and takes out Anthony Morales! Nice one!" said an emcee.

"Come *on*," Cage said. He wasn't whining, but he was getting there.

"Fine." Cèsar shoved his finger into the crack Cage had found. "You might want to back up."

He let out the cat.

Cèsar's true form was bigger than most towns in Alaska. When he expanded, it was in ripples of winter's power, nearly rivaling that of his sister who was once Queen. He held nothing back.

His form smashed Cage into the wall—*oops*—but then it smashed the walls open too, stretching through the so-called meta-wards with a burn that felt like his skin might flay itself. The rocks crumbled. Mortar turned to dust.

He knew he was ripping other cells open too, but Cèsar was suddenly human-sized among the tiny ants of the Army of Evil, and he cared about the ants about as much as real ones.

He swept a paw through the arena and took off its roof.

"The next fight's going to be a good one!"

They were still commentating. How were they commentating? Cèsar was escaping.

But then the world warped around him. It felt like invisible fists clenched around him—somehow bigger than the cait sidhe—and rolled him into a tight paper ball, shrinking him no matter how hard he fought.

He smashed to the floor in front of an iron grate, waiting to enter the arena.

The gate lifted. Cèsar was trembling, sweating, caught within his mortal form. He barely glistened like diamonds. Fritz stopped dead at the sight of him, eyes widening.

"Hawke," he said.

"Friederling," Cèsar said faintly.

"That is you, isn't it?"

"I think I'm actually ground beef now, thanks," he said. He couldn't even reach his sidhe powers again. It felt as though a schoolyard bully dangled them above his head, just out of reach, laughing at him for his attempt at escape.

The corner of Fritz's mouth lifted in a smirk. "The peak of your powers is...not what I expected."

"There's a lot of life after what you've lived," Cèsar groaned.

The announcers' voices resonated through the arena. "The next fight is between Cèsar Hawke and Shatter Cage! Cèsar is the brother to the Queen of the Winter Court, and a cait sidhe who is capable of —well, you saw what he can do!" Flora said.

The whole arena was crumbling and it was like nobody even *cared*.

Cèsar barely cared, getting a heartbeat to grab Fritz's hand and feel his warmth and solidness.

"Try not to win this fight," Fritz said dryly. "I'm certain I won't be able to defeat you in the next battle."

Cèsar and Cage stumbled into the heart of the arena. He'd torn the roof down as a cait sidhe, exposing a glassy night sky that shimmered with magic. The stands were filled with rubble, but it didn't look like anyone had died. The Army of Evil had just moved seats.

Cage greeted his opponent by saying, "That escape sucked. I'm moving to Plan B."

"Killing me?" Cèsar asked.

"If you'll hold still long enough for it." Flame licked over his fingers fresh. Cèsar had weakened himself, but Cage was still strong.

The emcees continued. "The opponent is Shatter Cage, a Hero, Messenger, and legendary thief from the time of CYCNUS! This is a rare one, folks. You're not going to believe what animal he changes into," said Louise.

"I turn into a phoenix, to be clear," Cage said, loudly enough for everyone to hear.

Now it felt like Cèsar couldn't turn into anything. He was so weak from his escape attempt.

And now he had no opportunity to try again. The audience cheered.

"Fight!"

7

If Ofelia had her way, she'd have stayed in her broken cell to watch Cèsar and Cage fight. Cèsar was everything that the announcers said and more, but he also had a skull thicker than most bank vault doors. A phoenix and cait sidhe weren't far apart on the food chain. And ice, like Cèsar, never did well against fire.

Her companion in the cell was much more practical.

"Come on," said Suzume Takeuchi, grabbing Ofelia's arm to drag her outside. Cèsar had shattered the cell's walls with his animal form. He'd failed to escape, but they still stood a chance.

"But Cèsar," Ofelia said.

"We can't help him if we're dead," Suzy said. She was as logical as her angel-blood dictated. They were sisters-in-law, so it was perverse for the emcees to expect them to kill each other.

Yes, they'd fought about normal in-laws issues, like whose castle they would use over the holidays. But Ofelia had only considered strangling Suzy two or three times, and never acted on it.

The angel tucked her wings so that she could fit easily through the halls they raced down. They were built of gray stone, like a dungeon, with actual flame torches on the walls that somehow produced no smoke. All of the cells where competitors were held seemed connected by that rear hallway.

Even when Ofelia couldn't see what was happening, she could hear thudding as Cèsar transformed once more. Suzy would have looked calm to anyone else. But Ofelia could tell that she was pale, worried about her husband.

"Something strange is going on here," Ofelia said, glancing through another shattered wall. Cèsar swelled, his crystalline flesh gleaming with all the glory of the Winter Court. Flame leaped from a figure Ofelia couldn't see.

"You're telling me," Suzy said. "These assholes scooped me from Dilmun."

Ofelia let out a surprised gasp. Dilmun was in the Ethereal Levant, with every ward their mages could muster. "How could they? Literally, how?"

"I'll figure it out," Suzy said. "And then I'll rip

their heads off and shove them where the sun doesn't shine."

The hallway sloped upward as they continued to run. They passed a blond woman holding a black cat in her arms, stepping out of a broken cell. She looked even more confused than Ofelia felt.

"Um," she said, "hello. Are you good guys, or...?"

"I'm an angel," Suzy said.

"Okay," the blond said. "That doesn't tell me anything."

"We're not interested in hurting you," Ofelia said. It was explanation enough. More people considered angels and the Winter Court bad guys than the other way around. But they weren't going to harm some girl and her cat.

"Cool. I'm Betty Beatty, and you are…?"

"In a hurry," Suzy said.

Screeches echoed throughout the arena. Ofelia leaped into Betty's cell to look out. Cèsar's enormous paw had smashed something flat to the ground, and there was no fire. She couldn't even see what form Shatter Cage had taken. He was now a smear.

Cèsar was so big that he pressed huge against the inside of the wards containing the arena. His bulk extinguished the basins of flame, smothering the stands in darkness so that only starlight shined upon them.

"Quick, keep going," Ofelia said, pushing Suzy up

the hall again. "I think we're near the announcers' box. If we can get up there..."

"I guess I'll find my own way out!" Betty called from below. The cat yowled.

There was a heavy wooden door at the top of the hall. Suzy leaned back and kicked it—hard. The wood shattered. She shoved the splinters aside and stormed into the announcer's box, where Flora and Louise lounged on a pair of thrones decorated in skulls. Their feet were getting rubbed by nubile servants with more muscle than clothes.

"Oh, that's one I didn't expect," Flora said, popping grapes into her mouth. "You guys are up next."

Ofelia materialized a spear of ice from her fingertips, swinging it to aim the point at Louise's throat. "Let us all out of here."

Pop.

Cèsar returned to his human size. He was on hands and knees in the heart of the arena, looking all the more exhausted. He shined with sweat, not magic. He fell onto his side.

A spotlight shined onto him.

"I can fireball him to oblivion if you don't let my associate go," Flora said.

"If you think threatening Cèsar's life is going to make us wimp out, you're wrong," Suzy said, arms folded, truly unimpressed. "You said yourself that anyone who dies here goes back to normal. Fine. Kill him. I'm still going to make you little weasels squeal and get home before I miss my soaps."

"Should we let them go?" Louise asked.

"Nah," Flora said.

Ofelia surged with anger. She thrust the spear into Louise's throat—but it passed through her to sink into the chair like she was only a ghost.

She *was* a ghost. Ofelia swiped at her shoulders and found nothing but air. Even the oiled nubile servants were an illusion.

"We put twenty heroes in one spot to battle to the death," Flora said. "We're not going inside too! That'd be a recipe for disaster." She laughed, tossing another grape into the air to catch it in her mouth.

Her jaw snapped shut. Ofelia blinked. When her eyes opened, she stood on the other side of a grate, waiting to enter the arena. Just like every other contestant had.

There was no escaping it.

The battles were as inevitable as death, and when her door opened, her legs moved of their own volition to propel her into the ruined arena. The illusion of an Army was still enjoying themselves. Suzy looked even more annoyed, which shouldn't have been possible.

"Our next challengers have some spirit all right," Flora said. "The short one is Ofelia Hawke, Queen of the Winter Court! The even shorter one is Suzume Takeuchi, a High Mage from Dilmun! Both of them have a lot of power and terrible attitudes."

"Just the way we like them," said Louise fondly, as if Ofelia hadn't made a sincere attempt on her life.

Suzy stretched out her wings, mouth folded into a severe frown, cracking her knuckles.

Ofelia materialized another ice spike.

"Fight!"

8

Ofelia Hawke attacked much faster than Suzy expected. Suzy had spent plenty of time training with the Ethereal Army and learned that her body was capable of feats that humans couldn't dream of, with or without her wings out. Few humans could have matched her.

But then again, Ofelia Hawke wasn't human.

She sliced across the arena and gashed open Suzy's flank. The angel barely felt it. The blade was so cold, it numbed as it cut. Suzy gripped Ofelia's arm and swung her into a chokehold. She bowed the Winter Queen backward, driving a knee into her spine.

"Kill me," Ofelia whispered. Her breath was as chilly as the wind off the icy fortifications of Niflheimr.

"What?" Suzy whispered back.

Ofelia drove her elbow into Suzy's gut, knocking her off. She spun a high kick. The queen had no right to strike so high, so quickly; Suzy wasn't prepared to take a platform boot to the face. She threw herself backward and flared her wings to gain altitude. She needed space to dodge. To think.

"Something's going on here, and they're lying to us," Ofelia muttered. Suzy could still hear it. Her senses were so acute that she could now hear the faint humming of charms projecting the Army of Evil into the stands. "I don't think people are dying-dying. Kill me. I want to find out."

Suzy created a seal of power, just in time to block Ofelia's hurled ice spears. They exploded into shards. "You might just die-die."

"It happens," Ofelia said.

She wasn't wrong. In Suzy's timeline, Ofelia had been dead for decades. She'd been killed by Everton Stark, one of the earlier competitors who met justice. She clearly had no idea what was destined to happen to her. She was still bright-eyed, youthful, and alive, and Suzy didn't want to hurt her.

The angel landed to exchange a flurry of blows. She wasn't trying to hold back, but Ofelia always had a blast of ice where Suzy tried to hit, and she was impossible to reach.

"One of us has to die anyway," the queen added.

Blades of their magic locked—ice against light-ning, sidhe against ethereal, queen against seraphim mage.

"I can come back," Suzy said. "I'm an angel. We've got tricks. Kill me."

"Either way," Ofelia said through her teeth. She shoved Suzy back with an explosion of ice crystals from the floor, shoving her into the air. "Whoever survives, whoever dies, we're gonna get everyone out."

Betty Beatty had been running for a good fifteen minutes and didn't seem to have made it anywhere. She'd gone down two flights of stairs but found herself in deeper tunnels. Anyone else who escaped must have gone up instead of down. She was completely alone, aside from the fat black cat who seemed perfectly happy to be carried. He was purring. He might have been asleep.

"Don't worry," she whispered to him, leaning against the wall to catch her breath. The stadium above thrummed again. She scratched his chin. "I'm sure you're not intended to compete. I don't know how you got into my cell, but you're perfectly safe."

Another boom. The announcers' voices were

muffled through the walls, but Betty could still make out the words, they were so loud.

"That was close! Suzy nearly took Ofelia's head off, but an ice blade to the heart stopped that!"

"Ouch. That's gotta hurt! Guess you can't make an ethereal omelet without cracking a few breast-bones, though."

"Gods, that's a bad one, Louise…"

"Oh no." Betty took off again, panting hard.

She had no idea how she'd survive fighting someone. She was a witch—but not a great one. She'd need an hour to light a candle. So her enemy would have to be a really slow, highly flammable creature without a survival instinct.

Or she had to avoid fighting completely.

A doorway appeared down the hall. Betty gasped, setting the cat down so she could run over to grab the handle. It was unlocked. She threw it open—

—and found herself on the other side of an iron grate, looking into the arena as Suzy's angel body vanished. Ofelia Hawke limped to the other side. She was clutching her shoulder, pouring magic and ice in her trail.

Betty was so shocked that she didn't move, even when her gate opened. Sure, it was surprising to get dropped into the arena. But what she'd seen behind the hallway door had been a *lot* weirder. Betty wasn't sure if she'd been hallucinating the scene on the other side. Or, more importantly, the people who'd been attending it—people who should have been dead, like Shatter Cage.

She stepped out, feeling numb. The fires around the arena flared bright as the other door opened. Betty couldn't see who she was fighting.

"And here are our next contestants!" Flora was practically hanging off the balcony to watch. "Betty Beaty, a pre-Genesis witch trained by the great James Faulkner himself!"

"And Mr. Poe, my personal favorite, the world's greatest detective!" said Louise. Her tortoiseshell kitten purred loudly and nuzzled her cheek.

Betty turned to face this detective.

The fat black cat came strolling out of the door, and he sprawled across the stone to lick his paw. Nobody followed him. It was just the cat.

"Wait," Betty said. "That's Mr. Poe? I'm supposed to kill a cat? I can't kill a cat!"

The audience laughed, those sadists. And Flora was the one who declared, "Fight!"

9

Lincoln Marshall and Dana McIntyre hadn't bothered trying to escape when Cèsar jarred their cell. The cait sidhe had made hole big enough that Lincoln could have squirmed through and unlocked the door for Dana from the outside. But why? So far, he hadn't seen anything that suggested an escape. Everyone who was due to fight got into that arena, and for one reason another, they fought. Neither he nor Dana were the type were to deny the inevitable.

So they just sat on the half-wall overlooking the arena, sharing the bag of candy corn that had been in Lincoln's pocket when he was abducted.

It was nice sitting with Dana like this. Lincoln hadn't paid a visit to the era of her life lately, and he missed the no-nonsense simplicity of his protege.

His first protege. The first punk kid he took under his wing, trained in triadism and fighting, and released into the wild to save the day. She was unlike anyone else Lincoln worked with. Like a crocodile, she was so evolved to do the one job she cared about —killing—that she had never changed much. She had a plan. She executed it. She got to the next thing.

Later, Lincoln would have to fight her, and Dana would plan to kill him.

The only thing right now was candy corn.

Dana surveyed him out the corner of her eye. "When'd they yank you from? You're old."

"I dunno, I don't bother with years anymore," Lincoln said. "You're not old."

She shrugged. "Doesn't get better than this." She'd been transported to the arena wearing full stone armor. Lincoln recognized the set. It was one that had been enchanted by her sister Marion to be lightweight and capable of enduring any physical attack. She even had a helm under one arm.

Dana plucked another candy corn out of his bag and chewed.

When Betty and Mr. Poe entered the arena, Dana noticed first. She guffawed, rocking back on her butt and kicking her legs.

"A cat! Linc, you see that? A cat?"

What Lincoln saw was a beautiful blond woman he hadn't seen in half a lifetime. Betty Beaty was gorgeous by any standard. Curves in all the right places. Kindness in her smile. Lincoln was older than ever but Betty remained frozen in time in her buxom youth.

"Yeah, I see the cat," he said. He tossed another candy corn in his mouth, feeling heavy and sad. He was going to watch Betty die, just like he'd watched so many other great people die in the arena, for no reason except to entertain. It was senseless. Ridiculous. "Cat's gonna win."

"Yeah? The cat washing its butt?"

"Yeah," Lincoln said. Betty wasn't a killer, and her opponent wasn't just a cat. If he had half the instincts of his breed, he'd toy with her until he was bored then bite her head off.

At least the candy corn was good.

"I'm gonna kill you, by the way," Dana said. "I always wanted to see which of us is better."

He shrugged. "All right."

Betty, meanwhile, was standing agape, flabbergasted by the cat that continued to ignore her. The Army of Evil was laughing in the stands. Nothing was happening.

The blond said, "I seriously can't kill a cat, you guys. This is ridiculous." She'd turned to appeal to the emcees, arms spread in surrender. "I'm a witch. Can you give me ritual supplies? And someone to fight who *isn't* a cat?"

While she was distracted, the cat stood up, yawned, stretched. Then he became a human.

"See," Lincoln said, popping candy into his mouth, "I told you. The cat's gonna win."

"The cat's gonna win," Dana agreed.

In his human form, Mr. Poe was a distinguished young man with skin as black as his fur. His hair was trimmed short. His goatee was groomed into a point. He had a pocket watch that gleamed with new magic.

"Expecting me to kill some adorable cat is sadistic, even for this scenario," Betty said, oblivious to the feline's change. "I really bonded with him in that cell. He was purring a lot. I think he likes me as much as I like him, and this is crazy to even say, because he's a *cat*. I shouldn't need a beautiful budding friendship to make murdering a *cat* horrifying to you."

Betty looked inclined to keep ranting, but Mr. Poe stepped up silently behind her and tapped her neck.

She crumpled. Instant.

"She's dead," he announced, "in case that's not clear." He polished his fingernails on his vest, which he matched with slacks and work boots.

"At least Betty died fast," Lincoln muttered to Dana.

He was trying to keep the tone light, but Dana

had been his protege too long to fall for it. She rested a heavy gauntleted hand on his shoulder. It was silent comfort. "I'm still gonna kill you, even if you're moping," she said. And that was another kind of comfort. The kind that made Lincoln grin.

Right before they materialized on opposite ends of the arena.

Lincoln had rolled through the universe in enough eras and places that he wasn't jarred by one more little teleportation. He was practiced in taking quick inventory of his new surroundings: the plain cell, the iron grate door, the arena outside.

Mr. Poe strolled through Lincoln's door when it opened. "Hello again," he said. "Lovely to see you, though I suppose it's not lovely here, is it?"

Lincoln grunted. He hadn't met Mr. Poe yet, but that didn't mean he wouldn't. "Feeling any guilt for what you did to Betty?"

"I'm a cat," Mr. Poe crisply informed him.

He vanished, pulled wherever the emcees wanted him next.

Lincoln stepped into the arena to meet Dana at the center.

"Our next challengers are like master and padawan," Flora said. "That's a Star Wars reference fo you luddites. Teacher and student! Lincoln Marshall, Triadist Brother, and Dana McIntyre, Las Vegas's least favorite vampire hunter!"

"Hey," Dana protested, jamming her helm into place. "Everyone loves me. Give me some love!" It was an order, not an invitation, which she turned on the audience.

Lincoln dropped his jacket and drew his blade. "I'm ready when you are."

"Fight!" roared Louise.

10

Dana McIntyre had faced few problems that couldn't be solved with a stone gauntlet in the face.

Lincoln Marshall took the punch as well as anyone could. He'd been expecting it and dodged, meaning she caught him with a knuckle, which was still enough to snap his head back. That would send him reeling all right.

Marion's electricity charm hadn't fired, though. Her armor wasn't working right.

And Lincoln wasn't someone easy to hit twice.

"Holy shit," Dana said when she suddenly found herself deflecting a knife blow toward her armpit.

Lincoln's other fist came around. He jabbed her hard in the soft spot under her other arm, slid behind her, and yanked one of the many leather straps.

Dana's right pauldron fell. He picked it up and swung.

He'd have clobbered her in the head if she didn't drop to the ground.

Lincoln was gray, grizzled, and had the body composition of beef jerky. He looked to have only gotten stronger with age, the way that old men sometimes did. Time had simply burned away the unnecessary parts of him. And somehow, this old bastard was *fast*.

His foot lashed out. Dana seized his ankle and wrenched, hurling him down. She rolled her weight atop him, and she managed to punch him twice in his old-man face before she felt the sting.

Dana looked down. He'd stuck the dagger in her side.

"Hey," she protested. She was bleeding. That *hurt*.

"When do you start killing me?" Lincoln asked. Blood ran from his nose, and he gave her a ghost of the smile he used to have. He'd never smiled much. That was a fond smile, like they were just training again, practicing the deadly art of brawling.

It lasted about a millisecond before he punched.

* * *

"They aren't dying, you say?" asked Sophie Keyes. She was an elderly woman who looked as though she should have fit into Isobel Stonecrow's pocket, though realistically Isobel would have needed at least a Baby Bjorn to carry a small adult around.

Something about Sophie radiated pure innocence, if not naïveté. She wasn't concerned about the deadly arena where she'd been transported. She should have been.

Isobel Stonecrow was good with a knife, and Sophie looked like she weighed five pounds soaking wet.

Hopefully Isobel wouldn't have to kill the little old lady, even temporarily.

"I'm a necrocognitive," Isobel said. "That means—"

"You talk with the dead! Marvelous!" Sophie's eyes were magnified by round glasses, giving her a cartoon-like stare. She had a nice smile and nice teeth, for someone who superficially resembled a raisin.

"I can't talk with anyone here," Isobel said.

"They're not dead."

"I enjoy this theory. However, it's plausible that our hosts are telling the truth, and these people are simply returning to their original timelines. It's quite possible! Shall we test the theory?"

Isobel wavered. She hadn't left the cell yet, doubting it was possible, even though Cèsar had destroyed a few other cells. He hadn't managed to break hers. But she would have loved to know what was happening. "How do we test?"

"Simple enough. We find the survivors." Sophie pushed the glasses up the bridge of her nose and surveyed the rear wall of the cell.

As they spoke, Dana and Lincoln were bleeding. A lot. Considering the two were human, they were good at fighting while terribly wounded. It was a fair match. Isobel hated it. She may have been the "gentlest, sweetest death witch ever," like Cèsar said, but she *hated* watching people hurt.

"Is Lincoln dead yet?" Sophie asked, sorting through a bag at her waist. She came up with a ring.

Isobel peered down again. "I don't know how either of them are alive." Lincoln's face was covered in blood, but Isobel hesitated to say that. "Are you friends with Lincoln?"

"Oh yes," she said. "I know him well enough not to worry." She tossed the silver ring at the wall. It stuck and expanded into a mirror, which showed only the dimmest reflection.

"How'd you do that?" Isobel asked. "I've never seen magic like that."

"Oh, it's just this thing I do," Sophie said.

She waved a hand over the mirror. An image

resolved: a stone hallway, probably like those else-where in the arena. It only displayed for a moment. The old lady waved again, and the image rushed down that hall, peeking into doors and cells.

Ofelia and Cèsar were being held in a cell—and having an intense talk by the looks of it, though Isobel couldn't hear anything through the mirror. Elise and James, the first victors, waited in another cell, ignoring each other.

And then, down another door, there was the phoenix from the beginning fight. That young Black lady named Deirdre Tombs. She sat in a chair, holding a mug, and—

Isobel appeared in a different room.

"Ooh, that was brutal!" shouted Flora. Her voice echoed through an iron grate separating Isobel from the arena.

Isobel had been moved to a holding pen. She was about to fight.

"Did she rip his head off?" asked Louise. "Is his head attached?"

From Isobel's standpoint, she couldn't tell. There was a *lot* of blood. Lincoln Marshall's body faded away quickly. Isobel swallowed down a surge of bile. She had just seen Deirdre, alive and well, yet she doubted anyone could recover from violent decapi-tation. Lincoln was surely dead.

"Dana McIntyre wins!"

The gates rolled up. Isobel stepped out into the arena. Dana headed for Sophie's door, and the old lady still looked as bright-eyed and eager as ever. "You fought so marvelously!" Sophie said. "Can I touch your armor?"

"No," Dana said.

"Of course not! That's quite all right! Beautiful work, regardless, both on the armor and your fight. Really, I'm impressed with your brutality, I've seldom seen such a thing even in—"

Dana disappeared through the door, disinterested in Sophie's fawning.

The Army of Evil was cheering again, anticipating yet another bloodbath. Isobel burped discreetly into her fist. *Do not throw up where everyone can see.*

"The next fight features Isobel Stonecrow, necrocognitive who's survived death more times than I can count! Can you count, Flora?" Louise asked.

"I sure can't," Flora said. "But she's facing off against the last Historian—the Spellslinger herself, at the peak of her power—Sophie Keyes!"

Sophie gamely waved at the audience. "Hello."

Isobel felt as helpless as Betty being told to kill that cat—but Betty had surrendered to helplessness and lost. She wouldn't let someone sneak up on her.

Not even someone this cute. She would go down fighting.

Grimly, Isobel drew the knife from her belt.

11

Sophie Keyes was fully prepared to kill this necrocognitive. She was confident the death would not be permanent; her mirrors showed only truth, and victims of earlier battles were still elsewhere in the arena. What she loathed was the idea of *hurting* Isobel Stonecrow, a perfectly lovely girl whose only crime was catching the attention of a bloodthirsty army.

Thus, from the moment Sophie entered the arena, she began spinning spells to disable. Once she rendered Isobel unconscious, she wouldn't feel the death.

Yet Isobel wasn't prepared to go down without a fight. She drew her dagger and set her jaw.

"I can make this quick, if you'll trust me," Sophie said kindly.

"Ditto," Isobel said.

She pounded toward Sophie on bare feet, quadriceps flexing under her marvelously taut golden skin. Ah, to be young again.

Sophie's body was not so athletic. She flicked her fingers to plant a spell on the opposite end of the arena, and she teleported instantly. Isobel skidded to a stop and whirled, dagger raised.

"Damn," Isobel said.

She charged again and Sophie teleported again. This time, the necrocognitive anticipated it. She whirled. A tiny glass bottle flew from her hand to shatter at Sophie's feet.

Sparkling gas filled the air. Sophie's head swam at the scent, and she realized with delight that she was going to fall unconscious.

"Potions! What a cunning maneuver!" Sophie coughed and swirled her free hand. She made an antidote. She drew it into her heart, and her head cleared instantly.

Her other hand hadn't needed to pause, weaving the sleep spell. She shoved it at Isobel.

The necrocognitive stopped in her tracks. Her eyes rolled back. She crumpled like silk, spilling across the ground. Other potion bottles rolled out of her open waist pack.

The Army cheered.

"Is there anything the Spellslinger *can't* do?" Louise asked.

Sophie shot a scowl at the joyful audience. "I'm killing her, but this is wholly unnecessary. Consider my complaint officially lodged."

She plucked the blood out of Isobel's body and disabled all electrical impulses to brain and heart. The death was instantaneous. Isobel may as well have been transmuted into a mannequin.

Sophie's confidence wavered only a tiny bit, when Isobel's body faded away. *What if she's really gone?*

There was nothing more depressing than having to kill someone so young and lovely. No matter how many times Sophie did it, she never found it easier.

"Sophie Keyes wins the fight!"

The gate rolled open again, and Sophie shuffled back where she came from, with markedly less energy than she'd entered. Channeling power for a subvocal hetânâ was exhausting at her age.

"This ends the first round of fights," announced Flora as the gate rolled shut behind Sophie. "We're taking a short break to rebuild the arena. We'll be back with our next fights soon..."

Sophie sighed when the darkness engulfed her. She expected to be transported back to her cell, but instead, a figure emerged from the shadows of the hallway.

It was a member of the Army of Evil. At least, that was Sophie's assumption. This woman was dressed as one of them, swathed in darkness and cobwebs, with leather cuffs. She was a ghost too—a projection into this arena, rather than a physical body. Sophie could see through her to the wall beyond. Yet she showed none of the gleeful sadism of the audience. Her bright eyes were sympathetic, and the flow of red hair over her shoulders gave her the noble look of a lioness.

"My name is Dawn, and I'm going to get you out of here," she said.

"We'll be back with our next fights soon," Louise said. Her powerful voice echoed through Elise's new jail cell—one built of polished white bone, placed above the arena, and untouched by Cèsar's destruction. The emcees seemed near omnipotence, but they weren't taking chances with Elise and James.

Life would have been easier if the Army of Evil weren't also brilliant.

"They've finished with the entire first round of match-ups. You know what that means, don't you?" James asked. He had been seated in the opposite corner of the cell for hours now, and hadn't spoken one word.

"We fight next," Elise said curtly.

He blew out a breath. "Elise..."

"Don't," she said. "I'm going to win this. I'm going to get to the victor's circle and kill whoever's in charge."

James nodded, and he turned his gaze away once more. It was easier for Elise to breathe when she wasn't under the weight of his Husky eyes. Yet she didn't fail to notice the way he probed his many remaining tattoos, as if inventorying them. Evaluating them. Deciding which ones he would need to survive against Elise.

There was no doubt in Elise's mind that James would try. Pride wouldn't allow him to fail. It was something she used to love about James.

But now, when the next round began, Elise would have to kill him.

Ofelia Hawke didn't know many things about her situation, but she knew this: she was never going to kill her brother, Cèsar, no matter what these people did. Period.

She had already stabbed an angel to death, and she was going to have to live with the memory of *that*. Ofelia never killed people who didn't deserve it. Suzy hadn't deserved it. Her palms were still sweating, and the sweat crystallized at the tips of her long fingernails.

"Well, this is where it ends, obviously," Cèsar said with a shrug. "You and I aren't going to fight each other. They can threaten any of the surviving winners and we still won't kill each other. So I figure, we sit our butts in the middle of the arena. We wait until they get bored or we die of old age."

"That's a big-brain idea right there, I'm sure they'll love it," Ofelia said.

"What else am I supposed to do? Izzy and Suze are dead." He swallowed hard, throat bobbing. He was as frozen as his sister. There was no color to his skin, normally so glittery-bright.

"They're not dead," Ofelia said. "They just got set free."

"And Pops sent our parakeet to live at a farm," Cèsar said. "Jesus Christ. Maybe we should fight and I should just let you kill me."

"Shut up, stupid," she said.

Ofelia jumped when the a hidden door opened in the back wall of the cell. It swung open to reveal the last winner, Sophie Keyes—an old woman with huge eyes and a terrifying ability to kill swiftly. She was holding a ring pinched between forefinger and thumb.

"Hello there," she said. "I don't suppose I could interest the two of you in a jailbreak?"

Cèsar and Ofelia exchanged looks. They shrugged at the same time. That was how they had always reacted when their brother Domingo proposed another wild scheme, like stealing every Mac Book Pro from the Apple Store on Black Friday. This lady must have been more competent than Diego. She'd killed Isobel.

"Sounds good," Cèsar said, voice thick in his throat.

They were met by a red-haired woman outside. Not one of the heroes, but someone wearing leather and cobwebs like the Army of Evil. "Hi," she said, "I'm Dawn. Come with me."

"Wait, are we trusting one of the people holding us captive?" Cèsar asked.

"Yes, quite so," Sophie said. "She's a defector."

Ofelia didn't like the idea of it, but she didn't like the alternative either. "Show us where to go."

The four of them rushed along the hallway. It was so quiet that Ofelia could hear the chiming of bells in her skirt's filmy mass, and the rattle of beads in Sophie's belt. "The Army isn't behind this," Dawn explained as she hurried. She was so graceful that Ofelia found it hard to believe her feet were touching the floor. "And we're not all happy about it. We love you guys. We don't want to watch you die."

"How can you love us?" Ofelia asked.

"I dunno about you, but I'm *really* lovable," Cèsar said.

"There's no way they can know us," she said. "Do you know an Army of Evil? Because I sure don't. I've seen a lot of armies but no Armies of Evil."

"We've been following you," Dawn said. "There are thousands of us watching, all the time. We cry when you hurt. We cheer when you win. It's just...what we do."

"An invisible audience! Goodness." This seemed to delight Sophie as much as anything else. "So how do we go about escaping this?"

Dawn stopped in front of an archway leading outside. Her expression was drawn in grim lines. "We're going to have to take out the person in charge."

* * *

"Welcome back to round two!"

Flora's cheering voice was the only sign that anything had changed. Rylie Gresham had been sitting in the corner of her cell, waiting for hours, trying to pretend she wouldn't have to fight her mate to the death.

It was hard to pretend Abel wasn't her next battle when he was trying so hard to break out. An Alpha werewolf, even in his human form, had a lot of strength and rage, and Abel was focusing it on the walls of his cell.

Rylie hadn't told him to stop, though the thudding made her more anxious. Abel had to feel like he was doing *something*.

"Our next fight brings Elise Kavanagh against

James Faulkner—and that is quite a pair, don't you think, Louise?"

"Oh no," Rylie whispered. She bolted to her feet to look into the arena.

It was still torn apart. Nothing had changed. There was no sign of the combatants, just as there was no sign of those who had already died.

Like Seth. Seth, who had gone running for Marion when he died, rather than saying goodbye to Rylie.

He had left the sanctuary to attend medical school in Las Vegas, but Rylie assumed he would come back. He would become a doctor and run the sanctuary hospital.

She hadn't let herself think about what would happen if Seth didn't come back.

Rylie covered her eyes with her hands, smothering her vision so she wouldn't have to see where she was anymore. But there were no better memories within. She could only think of walking toward Seth at their wedding, wearing a beautiful gown in the snow, and then watching him die to one of James Faulkner's spells.

He went for Marion.

Someone Rylie knew as a child. Clearly no longer true. She was beautiful, mature…skinny. Rylie's human body had changed more dramatically in pregnancy than when she became a werewolf. She felt more foreign to her skin now than when she was first bitten. Her breasts sagged, her stomach was wrinkled.

Marion was a half-angel, eternally young and perfect.

Seth would never come back. Even if James hadn't murdered him permanently.

A warm line slid down Rylie's wrist. Startled, she dropped her hands.

It was blood. She flexed her fingers and her pinkie nail slid off. There was a claw growing underneath, and had been for an hour, and Rylie couldn't calm herself enough to stop it.

"Who do you think is gonna win?" Abel asked, finally dropping back from the rear wall. He'd failed to make any progress in breaking out. "Elise or James?"

"Elise," Rylie said immediately.

"You sure? James is scary. If you'd seen what I had seen him—"

"Elise," Rylie said again. "Elise will destroy him."

"If you're wrong, you have to do all the midnight wake-ups with Benjy," Abel said. "God, where is he?"

"Aunt Gwyn has him." And thank the gods for that one. Rylie was going to have an easier time letting Abel kill her, knowing that Benjamin would be safe no matter what. "She has Elisha too."

Abel frowned. "Elisha?" His eyes flicked over

Rylie's body. If he noticed the change in her figure, it didn't reflect in the warmth of his gaze. He always looked hungry when he looked at her. It used to frighten. Now it warmed. "When did you come from?"

"2019. You?"

"2016," he said. A wavering smile crossed his mouth. "So we're not done, huh?"

"I told you, I want at least five kids," Rylie said.

"That gets us up to four already." Abel looked pleased. Maybe even smug. His hand spanned her waist, pulling Rylie toward him. "Look, whatever happens—"

"Let the games begin!" crowed Louise, interrupting him.

The cell disappeared.

Rylie and Abel reappeared in a cage. She staggered against him, unbalanced.

Their cage was swaying at the end of a chain, suspended over a jagged stone island. Rylie could look straight down onto the new environment through the floor grate. The sky was filled with watchful stars—and the open chairs around the island's rim were filled with watchful Army members.

A hard wind blew, setting the cage swinging faster. Rylie gripped the bars. Abel gripped her, as if afraid she would fall.

"Scenery change," Abel growled. "Great."

"Maybe it is. There are no walls, maybe different spells..." Maybe a chance of escape.

Another of Rylie's nails fell out. She buried her face against Abel's shoulder, inhaling the scent of her mate. It usually calmed her. But even now, his solid, reassuring presence only reminded her of Seth.

He's dead.

Elise and James appeared on opposite ends of the platform, rising from below as if arriving to perform the most perverse concert ever. The Army sure cheered like they were rock stars. The horror unfurling through Rylie made her gums itch as her teeth loosened—a sign she was going to change, which she hadn't felt in a long time. Not like this. Not without control.

He's never coming back.

"Fight!"

James launched magic toward Elise. His skin blazed with the spells he had tattooed on himself, and he hurled them like fastballs across the arena.

But Elise had already moved, too.

She was as fast as ever, dancing along the edges of shadow to evade his spellwork. Elise couldn't seem to expand into her incorporeal form anymore. She didn't try to swallow James. If there was frustration on her features, Rylie couldn't see it from above.

"Still betting on Elise?" Abel asked.

"Yes," Rylie said. "I always bet on Elise." She balled her hands into fists, trying to hold onto her human form.

Half of her mind cried, *Don't change. They want you to lose control.*

The other half was still screaming for Seth.

James and Elise clashed at the heart of the new arena. She seized his arm to stop another casting, but James simply unleashed one from his throat, speaking a word of power that made flames swarm over Elise's skin.

The Godslayer cried out, burned by the light. Rylie shut her eyes tight. She tried to swallow her panic. *Our fight is next. I have to stay calm. I would never hurt Abel.*

But that wasn't true, was it? Rylie was the reason that he was a werewolf in the first place. She had destroyed his relationship with his brother, Seth, at the same time that she broke Seth's heart. They would never reconcile.

Her tongue running over her canines had made them fall onto her tongue. She was growing wolf teeth.

Elise's snarl made Rylie's eyes pop open again. Elise rose from James's fire and swept it away, her skin pallid and greasy, bones visible as shadows through the flesh.

Rylie didn't see the actual moment of James's

death. It was too quick, and the floor grate blocked her view. But when she heard James's ragged shout, Rylie smelled the blood, and she knew it was over.

She shifted herself to see through one of the holes. Elise stood directly below, James's body at her feet, and a bloody heart clutched in her hand. Elise's head tipped back. She met Rylie's gaze. Elise looked furious, heartbroken, determined—and she gave Rylie a small nod before tossing the heart aside.

"Wow, that was *savage*," Flora said.

"Not as savage as he deserved," Louise said.

The Army was delighted by this outcome. Elise stalked grimly back to her starting point while they cheered, her hand dripping with James's silver-tinted blood, and Rylie felt sick watching her go.

She didn't have to feel sick for long.

"Our next fight is between two powerful Alpha werewolves—and Alpha mates," Flora said. "Ooh, that's not very nice. Rylie versus Abel? Who planned these battles?"

Abel's eyes met Rylie's. "I will never hurt you," he growled.

Rylie couldn't promise the same. She lifted her hands to show him that she was losing her nails. "I don't have any of my usual control," she whispered back. Her heart was pounding a thousand beats per minute. "I think—I think they've done something. Do you feel it?"

Abel clutched his head in both hands. "We're cursed." The last word was more of a growl as it hit him too.

Rylie was already losing her human body when the bottom of the cage vanished.

She struck the island mid-shapeshift. Her bones cracked, popped, rearranged. She was consumed by the anger. It made her wolf leap out, and her wolf was far more willing to fight anyone and anything than Rylie herself.

Unfortunately, Abel was changing too.

It wouldn't be the first time they'd fought. It wouldn't even be the first time they tried to kill each other. But the helplessness of it all was brief—Rylie's wolf took charge, and it only saw another Alpha gearing up to attack.

Her wolf would kill. Abel's would too. And the Army was, as always, delighted.

Louise yelled, "Fight!"

Abel went into fighting his mate with a single thought: *I will never hurt her.*

Unfortunately, his wolf wasn't quite so rational, especially not under a rage charm. The animal was simpler than him. It ran on pure instinct. And when a whole lot of adrenaline was introduced to his system, those instincts ran toward the violent.

In some distant corner of his mind, Abel knew the brilliant golden beast on the other end of the stone island was Rylie. His mate. Someone he loved enough to screw over his brother to win her heart.

That distant corner was filled with wordless screaming when he attacked.

The wolves clashed, and only instinct remained.

It was too fast for Abel to respond to Rylie's attacks consciously. She could snap her jaws on one of his ears while a rear paw sought purchase in his belly, and by the time he managed to dislodge her, she'd already opened a wound on his flank.

He knew he hurt her. He tasted blood when he bit down, and the snarls that came out of him were echoed in her throat.

Abel was almost as fast. His wolf was equally brutal. And he out-massed her by hundreds of pounds, giving his wolf the power of a missile against Rylie's freight train.

It was impossible to tell who bled more.

All he knew was that one minute, she had him pinned, and the next, he was about to tear out her throat.

Rylie's ruff of fur was thick enough to protect her throat from first bite. But he snapped again to get a better hold, and he felt her pulse against his canines.

I will never hurt her.

It was a single, powerful thought that overrode the wolf at the right moment.

Instead of biting harder, he released.

The fight was over after that.

Abel felt the moment of death. He heard it too—a sick wet crunch and a blast of white noise in his ears. He also felt consciousness retreat as if it remained on the surface as he tumbled down a depthless well.

He was ready for the end. He had been ready for it since his first werewolf hunt at his father's side.

But he didn't expect the end to feel a lot like waking up in bed.

"We've got another one!"

Abel groaned and rolled over. The excited voice was too loud for his thundering head. "Shut up, God," he snarled.

"Chill out, the headache will stop soon," said a man. His hands were firm but gentle on Abel's shoulders, helping him sit up.

When Abel's head stopped hurting enough to see, he found himself facing his brother. Seth Wilder. Someone who should have been dead.

"Seth!"

Abel momentarily forgot every one of his hurts, physical and otherwise. Fighting his mate. Watching his brother die. Getting kidnapped while he was on baby duty with Benjamin.

Seth was alive.

He yanked his brother into his arms and gave him a bear hug. Seth laughed weakly as Abel pounded him on the back.

"You're supposed to be dead," Abel said, holding him out at arm's length.

"Rumors of our deaths have been greatly exaggerated," James deadpanned. The witch had stepped out from behind a pillar. He was holding a paper plate and picking cucumbers off a salad.

"What in the devil is happening here?" Abel asked.

Seth sat back on his heels, letting Abel see beyond him. They were in a comfortable room with fountains, planters filled with lush ferns, and several cushy couches. It was baffling to see that it was filled with the supposed dead: Deirdre Tombs, Marion Garin, and even Everton Stark, who Abel clearly remembered murdering. Yet they were not the most baffling features of the room.

Abel frowned at the tables at its center. He could smell pizza coming from the plates.

"Are those party balloons?" he asked.

* * *

"That's not pretty," Fritz remarked, watching Rylie gut her mate. Even a giant black wolf with thick fur couldn't conceal massive wounds. From the looks of it, she'd torn his throat out all the way to the spine. Abel was well and truly dead. Now he'd been repurposed as an Alpha werewolf's chew toy.

His newest companion, Elise Kavanagh, said nothing in response. Saying nothing appeared to be her catchphrase. When he had been relocated to the cage above this new arena, and the Godslayer joined him, he had attempted to get information from her. It was as effective as asking questions from the cage itself.

"Ooh, talk about a mess," Flora said. "Glad I don't have to clean that one up!"

Rylie was still shredding Abel's body, though it had long since gone limp. She didn't stop until the body itself vanished and she was left panting at the center of the arena. Her gold eyes rolled with mindless fury. Her fur hung damp under her chin, much more crimson than gold.

"I could use some of this cleaning magic at my place," Louise said. "I've got better things to do than scrub counters, let me tell you."

"I'm pretty sure that being an infernal warlord means you can make other people clean counters for you," Flora said.

Such casual banter from their announcers, even when the murderous she-wolf was still slavering before them.

"We must be next," Fritz said grimly.

Elise finally surveyed him. Her black eyes took in the sight of him from head to toe: a kopis in his early forties who just killed one of her known associates. Fritz was an excellent hand-to-hand fighter. He'd trained daily since he could walk. Against any other kopis, he'd have bet upon himself.

But this was Elise—not just the Godslayer, and a demon, but a woman formerly known as the Greatest Kopis.

Whatever she saw in Fritz, it didn't impress her.

"If you hold still, I'll make it fast," she said. To someone like her, that was surely a generosity.

"I'd rather go out looking like a skilled fighter who was bested by a more skilled fighter, rather than a coward who fled the inevitable."

"Holding still isn't fleeing." She lifted her hand to suck James's blood off her fingertips, dark eyes smoldering. "I won't let you injure me. I'm going to kill whoever's doing this to us, and I have to be strong for it."

"Is that meant to be some kind of apology?"

She probably wouldn't have replied, even if the bottom of the cage didn't drop out at that moment.

Fritz collapsed to his knees on the blood-smeared arena. It was smaller than the first, and he could almost make out the faces of the people watching from the stands. Perhaps if Fritz survived to the final battles, he might be able to look his tormenters in the eye before dying.

An amusing thought, considering that Elise landed easily beside him.

"Now, this doesn't seem like a fair fight, does it Flora?" Louise asked, voice echoing through the velvety night.

"Not fair at all. We all know how this one's going to end," Flora said.

So much for Fritz's dignity. "I'll have you all know I hold advanced black belts in several martial arts," he said as Elise slowly circled him, "and I have been known to fight dirty."

He didn't really think the announcers could hear him, or even care what he said. He didn't expect a husky chuckle from Louise. She was seated nearest the ring with her cat purring on her chest. "That's why we love ya, Fritzy," she said. "Let's even the odds a little. Sorry, Elise."

Light flared around the edge of the arena. Elise gave a shout of pain. In the light, she became translucent. Her moonlight skin turned to paper.

A faint electrical buzz hummed underneath him. Fritz lifted a foot to see metal wires embedded in the stone platform. They had lit and electrified the environment, which was pure poison to even a demon of power like Elise.

"No powers from Elise," Flora said. "That's a little better."

"I'm going to kill every last one of you," Elise said through her teeth. They were clenched hard. Fritz could see the muscles flexing through her skin.

"Now let's give them a weapon," Louise said.

A rush of wind swirled around Fritz, making the hem of his jacket flap. He squinted into he spray of dust to see that a pedestal had appeared on the far end of the island, a good two hundred yards from where they stood. A black sword was situated on it. Fritz recognized the two-foot blade with a single cutting edge as a falchion, which was a traditional weapon for kopides. This one looked special. It seemed made of stone and imprinted with religious icons.

"The Infernal Blade? You're really trying to get Elise to kill all of us, aren't you?" Flora asked. "We could have given these two a butter knife and it would have been both fun *and* safe."

"I just like having a good time," Louise said.

So this was Elise's sword, Fritz realized, which would give her an enormous advantage if she reached it first. She was still groaning on the ground, gathering her strength.

Fritz couldn't let her reach it first.

He'd already bolted by the time the announcers shouted, "Fight!"

1 4

Were she not in excruciating pain, Elise Kavanagh may have respected Fritz Friederling. He still wanted to survive. He dived for her sword, knowing he was still outgunned. But the only thing she could feel was fury.

The electricity made her muscles liquid. The light took away her connection with shadow, leaving her stranded in her pain. And all this was done to even the playing field...for this guy. This tall blond guy with triangular features and a human form that should have been effortless to destroy.

Fritz's hand closed around the hilt of the Infernal Blade, and he brought it swinging toward her. Elise dodged the blow with a shriek of pain. It whistled an inch from her skin. Its blade was cursed with Lilith's poison. One scratch and even Elise would turn to stone, dying of suffocation as her organs ossified.

Unfortunately, Fritz was very good with the sword.

He moved with the swiftness Elise expected from an experienced kopis. He went for the kill, aiming for the tender parts her electrified flesh so conveniently exposed.

Elise felt like she was oozing across the arena rather than running.

He managed to slam the hilt into her shoulder, and Elise was weak enough that it hurt. Fresh rage flowed through her veins. The gasps of the Army only made it stronger.

She twisted his wrist hard enough that his fingers lost grip. The blade fell.

Fritz was too graceful to be seriously injured by his own weapon. But anyone could be nicked by a sword that sharp. It nipped his thigh.

He caught the blade before it hit the ground. Elise had to throw herself away from him to avoid a final blow from her opponent.

Elise collapsed against the side of the arena. The electricity was too strong. Everything was so bright.

He advanced on her, sword in hand. "Demons," Fritz said. "You always think you're stronger than you are."

"Men," Elise said. "You always talk too much."

Fritz took another step—or he tried to. His foot slid under him. His leg had gone stiff.

Ichor spread over his clothes. It crept through his slacks, turning them rigid, and Elise knew that it would be infecting the bone underneath as well.

This kopis hadn't lived through Yatai's attack upon Reno. He hadn't seen what Lilith's curse could do. He was still naive enough to continue moving, as if this would only debilitate him momentarily.

Elise rolled away to let him fall on the ground.

Fritz snarled, eyes squeezed shut, as he gripped his failed leg. "What the hell kind of sword is this?"

"It's mine," Elise gasped, scooping it from the ground. It was solid. Heavy. The same kind of obsidian that Fritz had become from toe to hip.

"Oh man, Fritz Friederling taken by Lilith's curse," Louise said, her voice echoing over the hum of electricity. "That's a painful way to go."

It was surely worse that Fritz had to hear the commentary on his death. He was gasping as the stone took his organs, but there was still light in his eyes as the Army shouted over his slow expiration.

"Damn." He shot a last glare at Elise. "I should have let you—let you make it quick."

His final words.

She took no pride in watching her fallen foe. She hadn't wanted him dead any more than she wanted

Deirdre Tombs gone. She hadn't liked the feel of James's heart pulsing against her fingertips.

These were merely appetizers for the entree to come. For the moment Elise would face the person who orchestrated this senseless pain, and bring that monster down.

One more death was worth that.

"Elise Kavanagh wins another fight!" said an announcer.

She barely heard it. Elise staggered to the corner of the arena, escaping beyond the lights and wires before she finally allowed herself to collapse. She was a wheezing puddle on the ground. But she was alive. She had the infernal blade.

And soon, once she found the monster in charge, she'd have vengeance.

* * *

"Our next fight is a real sibling rivalry! Cèsar and Ofelia Hawke are about to go head-to-head in the arena!"

"The hell we are," Cèsar muttered, chasing Dawn up the stairs. The announcers' voices resonated through the air. They were climbing to the top of the stone island where the new arena waited, taking a back path that led them along the teetering brink of oblivion.

It rimmed the edge of the arena, with no barrier to keep them from falling off the stone island floating in nothingness. The starlight was a vast field. Cèsar wished he'd had a joint, because it was trippy as hell to see.

Dawn took them to a door set into the island. "Here's the plan," she said. "The Army of Evil is on the other side of this door. It leads straight into the stands, you see. And that's my plan."

Cèsar stared at her, waiting for something more cogent. But that was it. "You mean, we're going to kill them?"

"We're all observers. We can't *die*. But you can disable us," Dawn said. "Once there's nobody to entertain, the fights will end…right? It's the best I can do for you."

But would it be enough? Ofelia gripped Cèsar's hand. "I can do something with this," she said.

"I'm likewise willing to attempt it," Sophie said.

Cèsar thought it was an awful idea, but then again, he was never the brains of the operation. "I've got your backs."

Sophie opened the door.

They emerged at the edge of the arena. The Army turned in surprise at the sound. They weren't expecting the invasion. Dozens of them were lounging on comfortable couches, looking darkly fashionable as they drank wine and smoked blunts, and none seemed prepared for a fight.

Luckily, there was no fight to come.

"Freeze!" Ofelia said, flinging her hands out.

Ice swept over the audience. They were fixed in position, trapped within jagged cerulean crystals that glowed with Ofelia's power. Even Cèsar shivered at the immediacy of it. Not to mention the chill that rolled off of her curse.

"Nice," Cèsar said, plucking one of the blunts out of a frozen hand. It wasn't an illusion or a projection. It must have been a multidimensional blunt. He blew on the end to warm it. "Anyone got a lighter?"

Louise and Flora rose from their thrones. They had been sitting outside the ring of Ofelia's power, so they were spared. "Hello again. You guys are really stubborn," Flora said.

"You shouldn't be surprised when twenty heroes of legend will go to any end to rescue themselves." Sophie's twitched with the spells she was casting. It looked like she was working up something impressive—something that made her entire body shiver with power.

"We just didn't think anyone would take it this *seriously*," Louise said. "I mean, The Writer didn't think anyone would, and we trust her."

Sophie's fingers stilled. "The Writer?"

"Is it George RR Martin?" Cèsar asked, plucking a

fire charm off Sophie's belt. He'd spied it at her hip and she didn't seem to be using it. "With this much death, I'm thinking it's George RR Martin."

Flora shrugged helplessly. "She's The Writer. This was her idea. And I would love to let you guys out of this—I really would—but until she's done, there's only one way to end this. Every fight must happen. Either you, Cèsar, or you, Ofelia, will have to die in order to move this forward."

"I don't get why you're all so freaked out," Louise grumbled. "You're all gonna be fine. Jeez."

Cèsar lit his blunt and inhaled. The galaxy seemed to swirl above him when he coughed out the smoke. "We're done fighting."

"You're not done until she says you're done," Flora said firmly. "Seriously, you don't want to know what The Writer will do if you keep—"

Ofelia didn't let them finish. She iced them too, and they became frozen in their poses, looking only mildly annoyed.

Louise's cat escaped the Winter Queen's chilly wrath. She jumped to the floor and darted into shadow.

"Now what?" Cèsar asked, taking another long puff. They didn't have an audience anymore. They were stuck in their crystal, unable to watch the fights...and yet the arena was still here. Nothing changed.

"I guess we could go find the others?" Dawn suggested. "I didn't really have more of a plan than this."

A hot wind gusted over the arena. It smelled strange—poisonous. And as soon as Cèsar inhaled, he felt himself losing control of his powers. He looked at his hands. They were duplicated in a ghostly, silvery form, even though he hadn't tried to release the form of the cait sidhe.

The blunt rolled out of his fingers. The beginning of his high vanished, consumed by rage.

"Damn!" Ofelia clutched her head, cheeks gone bright red. Cèsar hadn't seen her flush like that since they were teens. That was a sure sign his sister was about to throw a tantrum, but a tantrum from the Queen of the Winter Court was going to be a lot more devastating than some punk kid.

"Oh, drat," Sophie said. "I believe we're dealing with a rage charm."

On the last word, the world swirled around Cèsar, yanking away the crystallized audience. He found himself standing at the center of the arena, facing his sister.

She didn't look like his sister anymore. It was like his mind didn't want to recognize her. This was just some woman whose form was as multidimensional as the smoldering blunt—her breath the gusts of winter's longest nights, her shadow as the dark of the moon, her skin cracking with ice.

Cèsar used the last of his willpower to try to run. He'd rather throw himself off the side of the island than hurt his baby sis.

Before he could reach the edge, a metal blade slammed into the side of the arena. It was huge. A sword blown up a hundred times so that it was taller than Cèsar. He tried to dodge around it, but another blade slammed into place, and another. The blades encircled the entire arena. There was no more escape—only swords.

They formed a wall that blotted out all view of the stars.

"I think we pissed off The Writer," he said faintly.

Then the cait sidhe erupted from him.

Ofelia swirled with magic dark as a winter hurricane. Her hair floated around her shoulders as she turned snowy dead eyes on him, lifting her fists with spears of ice.

She was the Queen of the Winter Court, and Cèsar was one of her denizens. He was turning into a massive beast as rage boiled in his belly.

Even though the announcers were no longer speaking, he knew it was time.

Fight!

1 5

Mr. Poe was not one for violence. It was distasteful, watching people seized by rage charms and left with no options but to shred each other apart.

That said, getting to watch two of the most powerful unseelie sidhe battle was educational, if not overtly entertaining.

Cèsar expanded into a ghastly feline that looked to be ripped from the galaxies themselves, sprawling over the island with claws that may have been large but surely were no sharper than Mr. Poe's.

It's a shame they didn't pit me against him, Mr. Poe remarked to his cage mate, a shivering werewolf who had collapsed upon herself in a melodramatic display of bloody despair. *I have long desired to scratch out Cèsar's eyes. I'm sure I could take him.*

Rylie Gresham, werewolf Alpha who had just slaughtered her mate, continued to shiver.

She was not in good humor—another reason felines were superior to canids. Those dog types were loyal. They had feelings. Mr. Poe was far too practical for any of that nonsense.

Below, Ofelia slung ice at her growing brother, spearing him in his paws, legs, and chest. Though it would not damage the sidhe within, it did force him to fall, bringing a head the size of a coffee shop down to Ofelia's level.

Cèsar swiped at her, but the Winter Queen only needed to gesture to disperse his paw before it could land. She was buoyed on wind that kept her gown fluttering and her feet off the floor, and she plunged into the semi-corporeal mass of her glistening cait sidhe brother.

The Queen will be a difficult one to beat, Mr. Poe mused. *Should she confront that demon, she may stand a chance of victory. Naturally, I intend to be the ultimate victor.*

Rylie gave a tiny whimper.

Mr. Poe stood and stretched to his full length, spreading his toes, lifting his haunches, savoring the hum in his muscles. He meandered over to Rylie and licked her nose. She was bloody, but the gashes on her face had begun to heal. It looked worse than it was. The pain resided within her.

He purred helpfully and bumped his forehead against hers.

Yes, he would have to kill Rylie soon. The fight below was progressing rapidly. Contained within a cage of swords, with Cèsar's power risen like an ocean to fill the wards with glittering ice, the siblings battled so viciously that they could have been rival toms trying to claim an alley.

Mr. Poe mentally noted their techniques: Cèsar's savage reliance on claws and agility, versus Ofelia's brute force magic she wielded like a sledgehammer.

He could take either of them, assuming he could also take this werewolf. The one whose face he was still cleaning. She looked like such a mess.

Rylie didn't react at first. But eventually, slowly, her eyes peeled open. They were golden bulbs filled with captive moonlight and sorrow. Her lip curled in the faintest snarl.

Mr. Poe puffed up, stepping back. He waited for attack.

But she just lowered her head again and rolled over. Rylie had been wounded gravely on her belly, too. That would take more time to heal.

He rubbed his flank against hers, turned within the walls of her paws a couple of times, and settled into a ball. He purred as hard as he could manage. His friend, Gwyneth, had told him there was scientific support for purring as a healing factor, and the Alpha needed all the help she could get.

Because, of course, he was going to utterly destroy her in their next fight. Somehow. He may have been the size of an ordinary house cat, but Mr. Poe still had yet to face an enemy who could defeat him. He didn't fear this sad, wounded werewolf. He feared nothing.

Well, except that damn vacuum cleaner. The vacuum cleaner could go to hell.

Without announcers, there were no joyful voices to commentate on the fight. Mr. Poe observed it through the gaps in the cage floor.

Ofelia delivered the killing blow when she gripped Cèsar's skull in both her hands. She didn't twist—breaking his neck would hardly do the required damage. But her skin and eyes flared with merciless power, absorbing the energy of the cait sidhe, and she took Cèsar's life force with it.

His feline spirit vanished. His sidhe body collapsed to the floor, then vanished too.

The queen was left standing at the heart of a wasteland of ice, and even the Army couldn't cheer to support her.

* * *

Meanwhile, the losers were having a pizza party.

It was hard to say if anyone was enjoying it, but Betty was as happy as she could be. They had chicken barbecue pizza and white wine. Not even the boxed stuff. From bottles. What was there to complain about?

"This is crap," Abel was snarling at his brother, Seth. "We're being exploited!"

"Yeah, but look around. They're not *really* hurting us," Seth said. "I'm feeling relaxed now, aren't you?"

"Of course *you're* relaxed."

Seth had his girlfriend at his side, some willowy model type named Marion who declined eating pizza. Skinny bitches didn't deserve pizza. They were nestled against each other on a couch as if they weren't inclined to ever live without skin contact again, and Betty was about to barf her pizza over it.

"I'm hurt by this series of events," Betty pointed out. "I was really upset when I thought I had to kill a kitty."

"Getting eaten by Rylie didn't feel real good either!" Abel snapped.

"Mine wasn't too bad." Deirdre Tombs was at the end of the same table as Betty, holding a half-eaten pizza in one hand and a glowing silver cube in the other. "It was fast, anyway. And I wasn't doing anything interesting when they grabbed me, so..."

"You can't be this calm about what they've done to us, to our lives," said Suzy Takeuchi. She wasn't into the pizza, but she'd made two bottles of wine disappear and was looking for a third among the fountains.

"I've died too much to care," Deirdre said, shrugging. She stuck the rest of the pizza in her mouth and the silver cube into her bracelet. It was some weird iron shackle that gripped her wrist. When the cube squeezed into it, Deirdre settled back with a sigh.

Everton Stark was stalking in the back of the room, pacing from side to side like a caged animal. Which he was, from Betty's understanding. She'd tried to strike up a conversation earlier and he just growled. Deirdre had warned her to steer clear. *Very* clear.

"Sometimes crap happens," Betty said. "Crap usually doesn't end in a pizza party though, so I'll take this."

"Hey!" A sharp voice from the beds. Isobel Stonecrow had been waiting over there, and now she bolted to her feet. "We've got another one!"

Cèsar Hawke sat up looking dazed. According to the others, he was a lovely shade of sparkling blue because he was some kind of faerie, though they preferred to be called sidhe. He was so cute that Betty could have died all over again. Being one human woman trapped among the preternaturally gorgeous was awkward.

"Took him long enough," Suzy grumbled, yanking a wine bottle cork out with her teeth and heading over.

"The point is, they've lied to us," Cage said. He was sitting on top of a table. He had eaten an entire pizza, which was impressive for a guy so lean. "They took us against our wills. They didn't return us to our lives when we died, like they said. So what else are they lying about? How do we know this is really the end?"

The truth was, Betty didn't know.

But there were more fights to come. More people dying. And every successive person who lost a fight was more powerful—like Cèsar—and soon, she'd be surrounded by the world's greatest heroes.

"I pity whoever's pissing you guys off," Betty said around a mouthful of pizza. "But I'm kinda looking forward to see how it ends."

The screen on the wall flickered to life again. It was a little thing, barely bigger than a phone, and all it did was display two more names.

Mr. Poe versus Rylie Gresham.

The next fight had begun. And all Betty could do was wait, eat pizza, and pray this wouldn't end in too much suffering.

r. Poe may have been barely thirteen pounds—a fraction of Rylie Gresham's wolf—but he was nonetheless confident he could win their fight. Brains were consistently superior to brawn. He had proven it time and again in his adventures throughout the Thousand Lands, battling the Hounds of Arawn, the Red-Scaled League, and the vicious Miss Draconia. Never once had he prevailed through force. Mr. Poe's victories were thanks to his superior mind.

He inventoried his surroundings as Rylie climbed to her feet. The new arena appeared to be in a pocket dimension, most likely offset from a gaean plane, which meant that gaean magic would be strongest here. That was a benefit to Rylie and Mr. Poe equally, as both were shapeshifters (though a cat shapeshifting into a human was advantaged at all times because he was feline at his core, rather than a frail and flawed human).

The relative smallness of the arena could be used to his advantage. Mr. Poe was agile. Rylie was too, but she would require more room to maneuver due to her size.

Unfortunately there was nowhere to hide. Mr. Poe could easily leap into the stands, where the Army of Evil appeared to have been hexed to stillness, but magic hummed between them. A ward would block the attempt.

His brain continued to whirl with calculations.

He could, possibly, slip through a gap between the wall of blades. It was unlikely that he would be permitted to go beyond that, but it would provide him time and distance.

Rylie was clearly subject to a rage charm, considering how she had eaten her mate. She would be compelled to follow. Perhaps she could injure her face in the blades, and Mr. Poe could blind her.

Of course, scent was a far more powerful sense for the hunting werewolf. He would have to eliminate that as well. It may not be a dignified move to spray her in the face, but, well, dying wasn't very dignified either.

Disabling her in such a fashion may permit him to jump on her. Perhaps get into her wounded belly region. He didn't have silver, but even an Alpha werewolf couldn't lose major organs and survive for long. So then all he would have to do was—

Snap.

Rylie's mouth snapped shut on him. Mr. Poe felt a moment of shock—a heartbeat to realize, *I should have thought less and dodged more*—and then he died.

"Nice," Dana said bitterly, watching Rylie swallow the cat whole in a single bite. "What a nice fucking lady." It was hard to reconcile this kitten-eating monster with the woman who was like Dana's second mom. She'd always gotten along with Rylie, but watching Mr. Poe die made Dana hate everything and everyone.

Dana had escaped her cage to watch the battle from behind the stands. Her view was good, so long as she peeked through the crystallized figures of the Army. She hadn't *really* wanted to see a cat die. But it was the obvious result of putting a damn cat against an Alpha werewolf, and morbid curiosity had kept her rooted.

One of the other combatants, Sophie Keyes, climbed out of the audience with a member of the Army who was unfrozen. Dana lifted her gauntleted fists.

"Please don't attack. She's helping us." Sophie lifted her hands in a friendly gesture and stood between them. "Her name is Dawn. She's a good one."

Dana dropped her fists.

"I have another idea to end this," Dawn said. "I know where The Writer's door is. She's usually understanding, and this isn't fun anymore, watching people I like dying, and—"

"Okay," Dana said.

She turned to march away from the arena. They didn't have much time. If her mental tally of events was accurate, she was due to meet Sophie Keyes in combat next. With the audience and emcees frozen, Dana didn't know when the battle would begin. They'd have to move fast.

"The Writer's door is that way," Dawn said when Dana started the wrong way down the stairs.

"We're not going there first," Dana said. "This 'Writer' is on a whole other level. We're gonna need help."

Sophie's eyes brightened with understanding. "Yes," she breathed. "Excellent idea."

* * *

Lincoln Marshall ate another pizza while the other

dead heroes argued saving themselves. He sat back with Betty with his feet up on the table.

"Do you think they'd notice if we just sneaked out of here?" Betty whispered at him. Her eyes showed no hint of recognition. This woman had been pulled from a life where she never knew Lincoln. That was all right. He was just happy to see her again, young and alive and as passionate about free pizza as he was. When she smiled at him, he felt like he was half a century younger.

"Those folks might not notice, but whoever's in charge will. They seem omnipotent. We won't get far."

"Then what do we do? Eat pizza until someone else attacks us?" Betty asked.

"Pretty much, yeah," Lincoln said. He grabbed another piece of chicken barbecue and dropped it onto her plate. "We'll just have to wait until something happens and react."

The door to the room exploded open.

Dana McIntyre stood where it had been, her fists glowing with magic. She'd shattered the door with a single strike. Everyone turned at the sound of her entrance.

"Something happening like that?" Betty asked.

"Just like that." Lincoln let his feet fall from the table. He grabbed his hat, jammed it on his head, and stood to see Sophie waiting behind Dana. Sophie gave him a little wave. His mouth twitched into a smile.

"What are you doing here?" Seth asked Dana.

"I'm getting an army of my own," Dana said.

She studied the room—an impressive group, to be sure. James Faulkner was brooding but still tattooed with enough magic to tear apart a city. Fritz and Cèsar were all the brains and brawn required to stop an apocalypse, if necessary. The black cat, Mr. Poe, was snuggled down angel Suzume's shirt.

And then there was Lincoln, of course. He had his own ways of surviving.

He met Dana at the door, and they clasped each other's wrists in greeting.

"Who's your new friend?" Lincoln asked.

"This lady here, Dawn, she's from the Army of Evil. She says she'll take us to The Writer's door." Dana raised her volume so the entire room could hear. "Anyone want to come get revenge with me?"

Everyone exchanged looks. Enthusiasm levels varied among them, but nobody looked happy.

"Sounds like a great plan to me," Abel snarled.

"I'm feeling petty," Suzy said. "Let's go get that piece of smegma!"

Dawn led them down a few hallways to the first arena, still a crumbling mess, and crossed it together. Almost twenty heroes meant a lot of people trying to walk at the front of the pack. Only Elise, Ofelia, and

Rylie were still missing, and without any obvious leader, everyone wanted to reach The Writer's door first.

Everyone but Betty, really.

"I got killed by a kitten," she confided in Lincoln, hanging in the rear with him. "I feel like I do best in a supervisory capacity."

"In your defense, Mr. Poe is quite the kitten." Sophie gave Betty an encouraging smile. She was the slowest of the crowd. The Spellslinger looked like she'd been pulled from a future time where she was too old to make it far without a walker, and she didn't seem inclined on enchanting herself with speed.

"Nice work back there," Lincoln told Sophie. "You were nice to Isobel. You did good work."

"Ah, thank you." She reached up to pinch his cheek. "Look at you, you baby."

He felt old as hell. "I'm just glad you're hanging in there when you look like you should have retired to the knitting circle, shortcake." And she was shorter than ever, so he couldn't help but grin at the old nickname.

Sophie beamed back. In that moment, it felt like everything would be okay.

Then the group arrived at The Writer's door.

It was tucked away, hidden at the bottom of a spiral staircase underneath the first arena. The door was tall as three of Lincoln standing on each other's shoulders. Its handles were thick coils of brass with skulls hidden in the swirling design.

There were many other skulls less hidden: the enormous ram-like skull at the apex of its frame, the gaping gibborim heads stacking the vertical columns, the art engraved across the doors. When they opened, the seam would split the largest of faces down the center, and Lincoln had the unsettling feeling that they'd find nothing but brain beyond.

"There," Dawn said, nodding to the door. "The Writer is somewhere behind that."

Dana lifted her fists, lighting with fresh magic. "I call dibs punching this crap open."

She approached with her hand drawn back for a strike.

"Ooh, um. Yeah. Please don't do that." The voice came from the ram-like skull at the top of the door. The jaw clacked along with the words.

"The Writer?" guessed James Faulkner, scowling up at it.

"Yes, hello," she said. "Good to see you guys. Wow. This isn't where I planned things going, but I guess that's what happens. I basically asked for it."

Dana balled her fists. "Open the door so we can give you what you're asking for."

Abel came up to stand beside her, swelling with

the energy of his wolf. Lincoln would have been sweating if he were The Writer.

But The Writer just said, "No, that's not gonna happen. I can't be done with the event yet. I'll talk with one of you, okay? But the doors won't open until either Sophie Keyes or Dana McIntyre are dead. You guys are next up on the bracket, and, well..."

The skull's jaw hung open when she trailed off.

Cold worry washed over Lincoln. Those surrounding them turned simultaneously to look between Dana—tall, muscular, armored Dana in the prime of her life—and Sophie—tiny, aged, adorable Sophie looking like she might die if she tripped on the stairs.

"It's not going to happen." Lincoln put an arm around Sophie. She gave a little laugh, as if he was being silly, and he ignored her.

"Look, it doesn't matter how this falls out," The Writer said. "Either Sophie or Dana has to die. There's a lot of you out there. I know a couple of you are jerks because I wrote you that way. If one of you jerks wants a chance to take me out, then you'll have to take out one of them first. Sophie and Dana can do it to each other. Someone else can do it for them. Whatever. If you want my doors open, you've gotta kill someone."

Lincoln was too old and too annoyed to be

cowed by even the most omnipotent force. "Nobody's gonna do it, asshole! Nobody here is going to do what you want! Not anymore!"

The Writer didn't reply.

In the silence, an uncomfortable sense of anticipation settled over them.

Deirdre Tombs was eyeballing Dana, even as Anthony Morales edged nearer to protect his friend. Everton Stark was sizing up Sophie like he'd decided his odds were best if he went for the old lady. Even Suzy and Isobel were muttering between themselves.

"Nobody's going to do it," Lincoln said again, with less confidence. His arm tightened around Sophie.

"There's only one way through the door," said Shatter Cage. "We all know what that means."

That meant it was time for one more fight.

17

Cèsar and Abel must have spent an hour trying to break through The Writer's door, but it was impervious to all attacks. The bones were rock-solid even against the blows delivered by powerful beasts.

Dana McIntyre stood back to watch, arms folded, knowing that it was no good.

There was no way this would end without death.

"What's on your mind?" muttered Lincoln.

"Murder," Dana said bluntly.

"Don't touch Sophie."

Dana blinked. She expected Lincoln to be on her side. He'd babysat her when she'd just gotten old enough to grow hair on her legs, and he'd given her whiskey from the Middle Worlds for her eighteenth birthday.

"Who's Sophie to you?" asked Anthony. He was older too, but not nearly as old as Lincoln. Anthony hadn't ever gotten to be as old as Lincoln. He'd died sometime before hitting fifty, and Dana hadn't seen his face in so long.

"That doesn't matter," Lincoln said.

"Considering we're making a life-or-death decision about *Dana*, I'd say who Sophie is matters a lot," Anthony said.

"I just know the world needs Sophie, and she'd never hurt Dana. Not in a thousand years."

"That doesn't sound like you," Anthony said.

"No, that sounds about right," Dana said.

It made perfect sense if Lincoln was in love with the old lady. *Cute.* Dana hadn't known Lincoln had anyone in his life except for the gargoyles that followed him into every battle and the monks who lived at his church.

She understood. She would have let the world end before she let someone hurt her wife, Penny. But this wasn't Penny at risk, and Lincoln was a big boy, so Dana would do what needed to be done and Lincoln could deal with it.

As nicely as she could, Dana said, "It doesn't matter who kills who. Everyone who's dying comes back."

"They were, until you broke the dead out," Lincoln said. "The Writer's getting annoyed with us.

Who says she's going to send anyone back to their lives? Maybe she'll just kill them permanently."

Dana huffed agreement. She didn't trust this Writer guy either. "So what's this talk we're having? You offering to kill me so you can save your precious Spellslinger?" She couldn't help but get sarcastic about it, but Dana felt a tremor of uncertainty.

Maybe Lincoln would kill her over Sophie. What a disappointing end to this bullshit.

Before Lincoln could reply, Everton Stark stepped up to them. He was a square man. Built like a pro wrestler. His eyes gleamed gold, his jaw was scruffy, and there was death in the liquid movement of his muscles.

"I want through that door," he said to Dana.

She cracked her knuckles. "You and the rest of us. Do you think you'll be the one to take me down? Because you can try if you want."

"Back off," Deirdre Tombs said sharply, wedging herself between them. Flame danced over her shoulders.

"*You* back off," Dana said.

"I'm not talking to you." Deirdre stared down Stark. "This isn't about you, and you don't get to make this choice."

"But someone *is* going to have to die, so can we hurry up with that?" asked Cage, the other phoenix from the earlier fights. He swung an unenthusiastic kick at the bones lowest on the door. His fire wasn't nearly as hot or bright as Deirdre's.

"Happily," said Stark. He lifted a clawed hand.

Lincoln and Deirdre shouted at the same time, moving to separate them. Anthony put a hand on her shoulder. Abel approached.

They had everyone's attention until Betty screamed.

"No!"

Lincoln leaped for Betty—and the woman collapsing into her arms.

"Oh my God, no," Betty wailed, cradling the old woman to keep her from hitting the floor.

Sophie was already dead. Fading magic sizzled at her fingertips, spilling onto the floor.

Swears and shouts spread through the heroes. An uneasy muttering. Lincoln stared at Sophie like he was the one dying, struck by a heart attack.

"Yeah, that's what I thought would happen," said The Writer, flapping the skull's jaw in time with her words.

"You're a fucking snake!" Dana shouted.

The doors opened as promised, revealing a dark room beyond.

The Writer may have been a snake, but she was honest. At least this time.

"I'm going to kill you," Dana snarled, shoving past the others to storm through the doors. She didn't even glance at Sophie. She'd done nothing to the old woman, yet it felt like the Spellslinger's blood was on her hands.

"Not without me," Lincoln said. He was barely a step behind her.

They stepped through the open doors, over the threshold, and—

The world vanished.

Dana and Lincoln reappeared at the end of a row of seats. There were only enough chairs for every one of the losers to sit, looking up at a stage in a tiny theater. It was even framed by red velvet curtains. It looked nothing like the room Dana had seen through the door, which meant The Writer was jerking them around again.

A new pair of doors served as the stage's backdrop. The horned skull was still at its top.

"One more time," said The Writer.

Smoke swirled. Spotlights shined onto the stage. It had been empty moments before, but now Elise Kavanagh and Ofelia Hawke had taken opposite sides of the stage. They looked like reluctant performers—not surprised to be there, but not happy, either.

Elise hadn't recovered well from the assault by electricity and lights. She was still weak and skeletal. But she also had the sword.

Ofelia, on the other hand, looked as miserable as

a woman who killed her beloved brother could be. She was clad in ice and spiders. Sorrow blackened the glimmer of her eyes.

It took a moment for the collection of heroes in the audience to react to their teleportation. They shifted uncomfortably, muttered. Betty barfed over the side of her chair and kept crying in the quiet.

"Elise as a demon with the Infernal Blade," said The Writer serenely. "Ofelia after the Hvergelmir Purge, before the War of Alphas. I'm going to put rage charms on them to make it fast. One of them has to die for the next door to open."

Dana surged to her feet. "And then what? You want us to all commit suicide so you can laugh behind your door, you ugly bitch?"

The Writer didn't respond to the insult. The skull opened its mouth one more time and said, "Fight."

18

It didn't take a rage charm to get Elise and Ofelia fighting. Elise had already made up her mind about what was going to happen.

Killing Ofelia Hawke was the only way through. And Elise *would* get through.

Ofelia Hawke had the power advantage now. The Writer had done well weakening her with electricity and light—weaknesses that weren't exactly secret, but so personal that Elise had to wonder. Did she know The Writer? Was this personal?

If she wanted to find out, she'd have to get past the Queen of the Autumn Court.

There was no telling if Ofelia's rage was from the curse or if she'd snapped after killing her brother. She rose on a pillar of ice, her hair blowing behind her, tattoos seething over her skin. The spiders scrambled out of her skirts to vanish behind her, as if trying to escape the attack before it was unleashed.

Elise was a creature of infernal deserts, dark and hot. Ofelia was. She was bright, she was cold, she was rippling with gaean magic anathema to demons.

If Elise let this fight linger, she wouldn't survive it.

Her eyes connected with Anthony's, in the audience. He was sitting with Betty. The sight of them together—Anthony older, Betty young—made Elise ache in her chest where a heart should have been. Elise could imagine losing when she was the only thing at stake. But The Writer had taken these people too. She could touch anything.

Hail pelted Elise's legs like golf balls, fragmenting to pile on her feet. Ofelia blasted them out of one hand in an unrelenting stream. A fire hose of ice.

Elise tried to scramble out of the pile before they could grow to her waist, but the higher she climbed, the more Ofelia piled on.

The chill made Elise sluggish. She couldn't feel her feet to balance. She slid down, and Ofelia flung a rope of wind that shattered the ice behind her.

Elise leaped—and Ofelia twisted—and when Elise tried to raise the infernal blade for a strike, she instead was struck by a hex.

Her right arm was encased in ice, instantly and completely. It was cold enough for Elise's arm to desubstantiate. She shriveled within, and the infernal blade fell to the floor.

Ofelia was bathed in winter, fingernails extended as she brought all kinds of cold hammering onto Elise. Her eyes had vanished from her face. There was nothing beyond but the endless night of Niflheimr.

Elise rolled, snatched the blade off the ground, and threw it.

It sliced through Ofelia's billowing skirts.

If the queen hadn't redirected it with the wind, it would have sliced her leg too.

Instead, the blade chopped through the red velvet curtains and embedded in the supports for the stage lights.

Elise threw herself into the falling curtains as Ofelia shot hail after her. She pulled the cloth around herself, ducked under the magic, and leaped for the safety of shadows.

Ice froze the curtain to the stage. Elise had to keep running without it.

The scaffolding above them was turning black. Lilith's curse had infected the stage by cutting it, just as it had killed Fritz with a nick, and the lights went dark wherever the ichor spread.

Still, the darkness retreated against the gleaming glory of the Winter Queen. She closed the distance toward Elise with her toes skimming inches above the ice.

The scaffolding cracked.

With a sound like thunder, it fell.

Ofelia looked up just in time to see beams of solid obsidian crashing toward her head.

Elise shouted and leaped away. She took cover in the corner, one arm shielding her head as the other hung limp at her side.

When the stage finally settled, the rubble was silent.

Ofelia lay underneath it, crushed from the waist up. Gemlike blood oozed from the pillars. Her toes twitched once, then relaxed.

Elise rose, wiping her wrist over her nose. She was bleeding amber. Ofelia's ice shards had torn her in a dozen different directions, but now the Winter Queen was dead, and somehow, Elise was still going.

She yanked the Infernal Blade free of the wreckage.

"Elise defeats Ofelia," said The Writer calmly through the ram's skull.

The doors at the back of the stage squealed open.

Elise glanced toward the audience—still seated, watching her, all of them grim. None of them enjoyed the fights the way the Army had. Then she headed for the door.

"Not you," said The Writer. "Dana's next."

"Me?" Dana McIntyre stood up. It was something to see her as an adult, so similar to her father with the bearlike build and determined features. She wore a lot more armor than her dad ever had, though.

"Rylie Gresham waits on the other side, and it's your turn to fight her," said The Writer. "Whichever of you two wins is then going to have to fight the last battle against Elise."

Which meant more waiting. More fighting. Elise was sick of it.

She tried to walk through the open door, but she met an invisible wall. She couldn't pass.

"It's almost time. Be patient." The Writer sounded charmed.

Dana climbed onto the stage. She took heavy footsteps around the rubble that had crushed Ofelia, her boots shattering ice on every blow.

It was sickening, but Elise wasn't sure if she'd rather Dana or Rylie die next. She didn't want to have to kill either of them.

"See you on the other side," Dana said.

She shook Elise's hand. Dana had a strong grip. Elise was proud.

She passed through, the doors shut, and Elise was left to wait on the ruins of the stage for the end to come.

19

Dana McIntyre walked into the room behind the stage. The doors slammed shut, leaving her comrades on the other side.

There was no longer space for an audience. The walls were close, the ceiling high, the dark room rimmed by columns. It felt like stepping into an abandoned boudoir.

"Writer?" Dana asked, stepping into the center of the room. She slapped the runes on her gauntlets so they flared with Marion's enchantments. Power flowed through her. "Are you here?"

Something shuffled in the darkness. It was too big to be a Writer—assuming the Writer was a human.

Dana turned, fists lifted.

It was the penultimate fight. Dana had a good

mind for combat and combatants, so she'd had no trouble tracking the progression through the fights. The only people who remained, aside from herself, were Elise and Rylie.

She shouldn't have been so unpleasantly surprised to see the wolf lurking in the shadows at the back of the room.

"Rylie," Dana said. Her voice broke between syllables.

The Alpha had at least four times the mass of Dana, armor included. She was tall enough to fill the room, yet sleek enough to weave between the pillars. When she stepped out, her paws sprawled out like bear traps.

"You doing all right there, Rylie?" Dana asked, taking a step back.

Rylie's golden eyes were dead.

If there was any of Rylie left inside the wolf, she had retreated to a place so distant and deep that she didn't recognize Dana.

Everyone knew Rylie's story. Her autobiography had been a bestseller immediately after Genesis. The Alpha had spilled her darkest secrets for public consumption—including the part where she had murdered several innocents while lost in her wolf. Rylie had the capacity to kill. She'd done it before.

She would do it again.

"Damn," Dana muttered.

She knew Rylie well. Through every year of her childhood since Genesis, she had summered at the werewolf sanctuary with her sister Marion. Dana didn't want Rylie to be her mom. But, most of the time, she didn't want Ariane as her mother either. That hadn't stopped those women from loving Dana as much as their other daughters.

Rylie had kissed Dana's wounds, even when Dana didn't want kisses. She had bought Dana flowers when she had her first period—so cheesy, so weird, so gross. When Dana didn't want to show up to an Academy formal in a dress, Rylie was the one who took her to get fitted for a tuxedo.

If she were in control of herself, Rylie would never hurt Dana.

Yet the beast prowling the room's perimeter showed no sign of that humanity.

Dana didn't know Rylie's wolf as well as she knew Rylie, but she knew werewolves. She'd had to take a few down when they got moon sick.

Werewolves were fast—really fast. They could shred a human being faster than a cheese grater versus mozzarella. Few preternaturals were as strong as werewolves. Even vampires didn't stand a chance against them.

Dana's armor was tailored toward fighting vampires. It made her strong.

Just not strong enough.

She threw herself toward the pillars, away from Rylie, before the wolf so much as twitched. Dana didn't see the swipe coming. She just heard the screech of silver claws against stone. She felt fire on the side of her knee—an exposed patch that sacrificed coverage for flexibility.

Rylie's claws deflected from the plates, but she still drew blood. It gushed within denim.

Dana slammed her back against the pillar, keeping it between herself and the wolf. She yanked a medallion from her belt and jammed it against her knee. It turned raging fire to relieving ice. Marion's healing magic was some of her best. Dana could heal at the speed of the Alpha werewolf.

The wolf snarled to her right. Breath blasted hot over Dana's pauldron.

She flung herself away just in time, rolling behind the next pillar when Rylie's jaws snapped on the first. The werewolf's mouth was big enough to rip half the pillar off. Dust exploded over the floor. It peppered Dana's knee plate when she jumped again.

Dana needed to generate silver if she hoped to kill Rylie, but transubstantiation was the slowest of Dana's charms. She would need a full thirty seconds before she converted one of her arm plates into a proper silver blade.

Dana ducked behind another pillar to rip off her arm plate, loosening leather straps with her teeth.

She smashed a transubstantiation charm against it. The plate turned white-hot—she'd melt her hand off if she tried to handle it.

Rylie leaped, swiping her paw at Dana's head.

Dana kicked the white-hot plate across the room and followed it, somersaulting under Rylie's arm. They were so close that the shaggy blond fur swept over Dana's spiky blond hair. She smelled Rylie's musk and Abel's blood.

She came up on her feet behind Rylie and swung both fists.

Her gauntlets cracked against the Alpha's skull. The blow sent Rylie to the ground.

Behind Dana, her arm plate sizzled with power. It had begun to change shape but not substance. It needed another good fifteen seconds.

Rylie snarled and came up to bite.

Dana lifted her arm to protect herself—her wrong arm.

Werewolf jaws shut on her exposed flesh.

Dana's mind refused to process the pain. Her arm became nothing from the elbow down. Rylie treated her like a rawhide, snarling and tearing, and Dana roared as she slammed her opposite fist into Rylie's eye.

The magic's sizzle turned to a hum. It was almost done.

Dana tore herself away from Rylie with a cry. She

didn't dare check to see how much of her arm was left. She extended her good hand to pick up the newly formed silver blade—

—but Rylie's claws sank into Dana's hip and jerked her back.

The world flipped. Dana ended up pinned underneath the Alpha's weight, like a tank was parked on her breastplate. Her fingers strained over her head for the silver blade.

Rylie's jaw snapped shut on Dana's skull.

* * *

Elise listened to the fight between Dana and Rylie from the stage, clenching her sword at her side, wishing that she could have broken through to them.

"Hello," Marion said, lifting her gown to her knees so she could step onto the stage. She was one of the only people who could get away with embracing Elise.

Elise hugged her half-sister back, tightly but briefly. "What do you think this is? The Writer?"

"I don't know," Marion said. "I know Librarians, Historians... There are people in charge of the meta-text of the universe. Perhaps The Writer is some similar force."

"Maybe she's like Q." Betty climbed onto the stage with them. She seemed to have made amends with the cat who murdered her, since he was purring on her shoulders again. No hard feelings. "You know, like on Star Trek? Q? This omnipotent chaos entity that likes to mess with Picard?"

"Why, hello." Marion extended a hand. "I don't think we've met. I'm Marion Garin."

"Betty," she said. "Wow. You are *beautiful.*"

Elise wasn't sure what she felt, watching her sister meet her long-lost best friend. It was almost impossible to watch. Like she was trying to look directly at the sun.

She could have lived in that moment, painful as it was, for an eternity.

But she was given no such time.

The room on the other side of the doors went silent. Within moments, Elise felt a jerk, the stage vanished, and she reappeared in the Library of Dis.

She stood on the crystal floor looking into the lower levels. The Librarians usually kept their desks there. Today, it was empty. The floor had been cleared of all but a single chair set back in the stacks, with a writing desk and a typewriter. Someone was sitting in that chair, but she was angled so Elise couldn't see a face.

Finally. The Writer.

Elise strode toward her. But she only made it two steps before Rylie blocked her path.

The wolf looked as rough as Elise felt. Neither

had been healed from their earlier fights, so Rylie remained bloody, ragged, wavering on her paws. The fire in her eyes hadn't dimmed. The wolf was still in charge, and she wanted to win this last fight.

Elise had to get through Rylie to reach The Writer. To find her answers.

She wouldn't back down now.

"Fight!" called The Writer from her desk.

20

E lise had always wondered who would win in a fair fight, if it came down to battling Rylie.

She wasn't sure that this was a fair fight. The Infernal Blade was powerful—so powerful it was much liability as asset—but Elise had been injured since her fight against Fritz Friederling.

Rylie looked injured too. Blood caked her fur into ropes that swung on every step. A lot of that wasn't her blood, though, and she would have already healed any wounds that caused it. Her healing was better than Elise's even at the best of times.

Elise had no silver, and there would be no reasoning with a werewolf in this condition, so Elise couldn't exploit Rylie's greatest weakness: the Alpha's tender heart.

That meant she needed to get close enough to stab Rylie with the Infernal Blade, and she needed to do it without getting mauled.

Rylie pounced at Elise without warning. She soared across the crystal floor.

Elise took cover behind a bookshelf. Rylie smashed into the other side, sending ancient books and scrolls to the floor. Her paws scrabbled for purchase against the mess.

The wolf got her footing. She leaped again.

Surrendering to shadow only allowed Elise to phase a few feet away. There was too much candle-light in the room. As weak as Elise felt, she'd have needed pitch blackness to cross the Library without becoming corporeal.

Rylie swung around to search for Elise, disoriented.

Elise hid behind another of the bookshelves and edged further from the center of the room. She got against the wall, where it was darker.

The werewolf was sniffing the air, trying to figure out where Elise had gone. There would be too many strange scents in the City of Dis for Rylie to sort them immediately. Once she pinned down Elise's particular odor, it would take seconds for this fight to end.

But The Writer was so close. *So close*.

It still wasn't dark enough for Elise to phase

against the back wall. What she needed was more strength. Her mind raced with possible food sources —Rylie, for instance, or The Writer, or some kind of artifact hidden higher in the Library of Dis—and then she realized she should have already been close to human meat.

Rylie huffed. Her golden eyes fell on Elise in the shadows.

Elise punched her fist through the stone at the base of the wall. A brick came loose. She hauled it out, spun the brick like a shot put, and sent it straight between Rylie's eyes. It pulverized with the force of contact.

The werewolf was stunned, staggering.

Elise had to be fast.

She dived back to the hole she'd made and reached through to the other side, praying that The Writer had prepared this world beyond the confines of the Library. She was rewarded by the feeling of dry, freshly churned soil on the other side. Elise swept her hand around until she felt the contact of human fingers.

The Flesh Gardens were outside, exactly where they were meant to be.

Elise yanked and twisted and sawed the hand she'd gripped, until a ragged stump came out of the earth.

Rylie had gotten to her feet.

Elise leaped into the stacks, taking the hand from the Flesh Gardens with her. She jammed its wrist into her belt so that she could climb the shelves out of Rylie's reach. The werewolf leaped and scrabbled against the shelves, trying to reach her.

It wouldn't take long for Rylie to figure it out. Elise leaped from the top of one shelf to the next while she began eating the bloody stump.

The taste of human flesh was unfortunately familiar. Elise had swallowed her fair share of humans in battle, and whether she was shadow or flesh, their deaths left the lingering aftertaste of sweet pork. The blood wasn't fresh enough to be palatable. Yet every ragged fragment torn from the bone to slide down her throat gave Elise new strength.

Her skin grew in opacity. She glowed again.

She ate what was left of the forearm, crunching finger bones between her molars, before Rylie managed to catch her.

A paw struck Elise's calf. The wolf's claws shredded through her skin as easily as the cloth, and she lost balance, falling from the shelves.

She tumbled toward Rylie's waiting mouth.

Elise phased.

She disappear and reappear behind Rylie, sword still in hand, and plunge the blade into the werewolf's back. Rylie roared and twisted to snap. Elise yanked the sword out to stab again, and again, and again. When the jaws came toward her, Elise hacked at those too.

Lilith's curse wouldn't turn Rylie to stone fast enough to neutralize her threat. So Elise had to do that, one swing at a time.

She kept cutting until all the pieces were black and nothing left could move.

The sword slipped from Elise's hand. It clattered to the floor of the Library, and she was only moments behind it, hitting her knees in a pool of Rylie's blood.

"Wow," said The Writer. She pulled the cord on her desk lamp. The shadows receded, revealing an Underwood typewriter, a stack of notebooks, and The Writer herself.

The Writer was a woman little older than Elise. She looked human, from her fair skin to her dark-blue eyes. She wore large glasses and an even larger sweater over leggings.

"Hi." She smiled awkwardly at Elise.

Elise didn't smile back. She stepped around Rylie's body to close the distance between them. "Who are you?"

"The Writer," she said. "I don't have another way to explain it. The title's pretty explanatory. I write...everything." She gestured in the general direction of the Library, and especially at Elise.

"Everything here came out of my head. It exists because I imagined it, wrote it down, and shared it with readers."

"You're a god?" Elise asked.

"No, I made those too," The Writer said. "I'm an author of fiction. We're in a book right now."

"No," Elise said.

If it were true, then this unremarkable human was responsible for everything that had happened in Elise's life. Every wretched moment. Not just the ones that had happened since arriving in the arena.

And none of it was real.

It couldn't be true.

Elise contemplated putting the sword into this woman's throat. "Why did you do this?"

"I wanted to meet you," The Writer said. "I can write a fictionalized form of myself meeting you, but there's more to a book than putting words down. Stories truly happen between the author's words and the people who read them. In order to be with you, I inserted myself into a project developed with the readers."

None of it made any sense to Elise. Yet she believed it, and she had never felt smaller. "This was how you chose to do it? By making us fight and suffer?"

"It's how I always do it," The Writer said.

This was beyond the pale. "I'm not some figment of your imagination!"

The Writer gave a pained little smile. "Except...you are? And you're not accepting it because that's how I've imagined you, too?"

"Was it worth it?" Elise asked. "Everything you've done to us?"

The Writer gave a self-conscious shrug, gaze fixed on Rylie's shaggy back. "Real people see themselves in your stories. I've had readers tell me that my books got them through hospital stays. People have tattoos of you on their skin—real people, with your faces on them—and they name their daughters and cats after you, allow you to exist within their lives. That means something. It wouldn't mean anything if you weren't hurting to get us there."

Elise had lost all urge to fight. The sword dropped to her side. "Then I'm suffering endless torment...not because an entire universe needs it. But because a few 'real' people want tattoos."

"You comfort people fighting their own battles, a lot of them worse than yours against His," The Writer said gently. "You can't get much more heroic than that." Thoughtfulness tipped her mouth down, chin wrinkling. "Can you understand that?"

The question sounded rhetorical. It wasn't something for Elise to answer, but for The Writer to puzzle. One more element of the character to weigh.

"Thanks for everything," The Writer said. She was so sincere, so *earnest*, that Elise actually cringed on the inside.

She didn't want thanks. Gratitude wouldn't change anything.

"Anyway, that's it. I just wanted to see you all together again, and now we're done. I'm writing myself out of the universe. I shouldn't be here. It's cheesy." The Writer sat at her Underwood once more. "I can't promise you happiness, Elise, but I can promise you contentment. We both know what you need. It's not a happy ending. It's better than that."

Elise took a step toward her, raising a fist. She wasn't sure what she meant to do. Exact revenge? Destroy the typewriter and end the story? Prevent The Writer from escaping?

She was given no opportunity to find out. With a few swift keystrokes, The Writer left her world and ended the scene.

* * *

Things were tense among the remaining combatants.

They'd been left with Ofelia's body, the wreckage of the stage, and questions that Lincoln Marshall preferred not to voice.

The Queen of the Winter Court's corpse hadn't

disappeared when she lost, not like the other fights. Lincoln wasn't sure if Sophie had disappeared either. He'd been yanked from that hallway to the audience without time to mourn.

Clearly, they'd broken away from The Writer's plan. What should have been a series of simple arena fights and a pizza party for the losers had led to a minor uprising.

What if they'd spent The Writer's goodwill? What if she wasn't going to bring anyone else who died back?

Sophie. Dana. Ofelia. Elise.

There were too many people that Lincoln wasn't prepared to lose. He'd encountered strangeness in his years of monastic service, but this was something else—stranger than the furthest reaches of the Middle Worlds and the things that mildewed in their depths.

It had been a long time since he felt so helpless.

"Want a beer?"

Seth and Anthony headed over to him with a six-pack. They'd already helped themselves to half of It.

"Do I wanna know how y'all smuggled that in here?" Lincoln asked.

"We found it under the stage." Seth sat in the chair next to him, passing over a fresh bottle.

Anthony propped himself against the edge of the stage so he could face them. "We also found a couple more pizza boxes down there. Seems like our cruel captor *really* wants to make sure we're eating while we're tortured."

"Great, my Aunt Bee's holding us captive," Lincoln grumbled.

"It's been a while since Elise disappeared," Seth said. He took a long, long drink of his beer. "What do you think happens once it's over?"

"They said we'll go back to our lives, didn't they?" Lincoln asked.

"I can't accept that," Anthony said.

Gods, Anthony was young. Seth was too. They hadn't spent nearly as much time fighting hopeless causes as Lincoln had. "If there's one thing I've learned, brothers, it's that faith can get you through anything," Lincoln said. "You don't have to have faith in the gods. You don't even need to have faith in yourself. Just have faith that the right thing is possible. Walk toward that future one step at a time."

"That's such triadist bullshit." Anthony shook his head and took one more drink.

"Triadists know a few things," Seth said.

"If everything happens the way it's supposed to, we'll know," Lincoln said. "We may not remember this consciously, but our souls know when we're on the right path. This may end at any moment. You will open your eyes on the life you're supposed to be living. It will feel *right*. You'll know."

Anthony blew a breath out. "Yeah, but what if it doesn't?"

"Then it's no worse than now," Lincoln said.

"You're full of crap, Marshall," Anthony said, "but it's reassuring crap, at the moment."

Lincoln was glad he could reassure someone. Even now, he was still just thinking about Sophie. Remembering Betty's horrible cry when Sophie took her own life. And he wanted someone to make him believe that she was going to be okay.

The lights in the audience suddenly went out.

Everyone around the room stopped talking, cutting off mid-word. James and Abel looked like they'd been arguing. Stark had retreated to a corner with Deirdre Tombs. The others had been loosely congregated, whispering.

The red velvet curtains came loose from their ties. They swung shut over the stage, tassels whispering over Ofelia's limp arm so that only one foot and dust were visible.

A single spotlight shone on the curtains. Confetti burst from a cannon concealed among the lights. A banner rolled down from the top—a picture of Elise, battle-scarred and furious. The banner claimed her as "Victor!"

"Congratulations to Elise Kavanagh." The Writer's voice was slightly louder than the pleasant music that piped over the speakers. "And from me to you, thanks for everything. It's been almost twenty years. I couldn't have asked for better company."

"*Thanks?*" Anthony roared, hurling his beer bottle at the curtains.

"Glitter," Lincoln said wryly. He'd gotten confetti and glitter dumped on him directly. It was in his hair, his lapels, his socks.

"That's how you know The Writer is evil incarnate," Seth said, brushing off a shoulder.

Lincoln reached up to shake the confetti out of his hair. "I think we—"

A few scraps of colorful plastic landed on Lincoln's feet.

Where did those come from?

He looked up. He was standing in the Holy Nights Cathedral, within arm's reach of freshly lit candles. It was lucky the confetti hadn't fallen onto the candles. Lincoln never figured out how to get bad smells out of the nave, and burned plastic was terrible.

"Did you make this?" Lincoln asked the cathedral at large, holding up the pieces of confetti.

The church gave no obvious response. It was slumbering, having assumed its favorite floor plan to settle in Grove County for the summer. The spirits had a way of going on vacation when Lincoln set up camp on Earth. He didn't blame them for being bored in Northgate; Lincoln still got bored in Northgate sometimes, and he used to live there.

"Where did the glitter come from?" asked Sophie, gliding up the aisle.

"I'm not sure," Lincoln said. "Wasn't you?"

"I have a serious moral opposition to the ubiquity of plastic." She pushed her glasses up the bridge of her nose, and it made her eyes momentarily huge. The glasses were a recent fixture. Sophie was a nerd who never got out of books, so her eyes were failing fast. "Ah, well. We can safely assume it's another quirk of the gods and forget about it."

That sounded fine to Lincoln. Actually, it sounded *great*. He didn't realize he was grinning at Sophie until she gave him a sideways look, hugging her journal tighter to her chest.

"What?" Sophie asked suspiciously.

He shrugged. "Nothing. Just in a good mood."

"You're excited to mentor another of Rylie's children, aren't you?"

So *that* was what he'd been doing. He'd somehow forgotten. It felt like he'd blacked out, but only for an instant—just long enough to reset his brain. That little blip had left him feeling cheerful and calm. Better than a whole year of sleep.

"Guess I am," Lincoln said. "Is he here yet?"

"Just arrived," Sophie said. "He's waiting in your office."

Lincoln followed her up the hallway, casting one last glance at the puff of confetti on the floor. The door swung open. Shifting air pressure kicked up a breeze, and the confetti swirled away into shadow.

* * *

Elise Kavanagh was sitting on a rock in the desert, sharpening a knife, and waiting for the sunrise. She had been there for hours. Nothing had happened during that time. She'd eradicated the daimarachnids nesting in the area, and kept up on extermination efforts, so there were few battles to fight in her territory.

On a downward swipe with her whetstone, she paused. She felt as though someone had pressed the pause button on her life and hit play again so quickly that she didn't miss anything. It was a jarring sensation, akin to deja vu, and Elise glanced up to search for anyone in her presence.

Anthony approached from McIntyre's trailer. His heartbeat pulsed on Elise's tongue for a full eight minutes as he jogged to reach her camp.

"Late night, or early morning?" Anthony asked, hunkering down beside her.

The sight of him relaxed her. "The nights are always late." Elise couldn't tolerate sunlight anymore. Even its reflection could burn her sometimes, if the moon was too bright. She was toying with discorporealization sitting outside for so long, but she loved the crisp cool of desert predawn. It reminded her of being home in Reno.

Anthony knew how much she loved it. They'd gone jogging more than a few chilly mornings together in Reno, back when they were young. When Elise was human. "I brought you a reflective blanket, in case you want to stick around a few more minutes without toasting." He offered it to her.

Elise curled her fingers around its edge and felt a foreign pang of sadness when she met Anthony's affectionate brown eyes. It felt as though he had died —or maybe as though Elise had died again. The strangest flash of a thought.

The moment passed. Elise gave a little shiver and flicked the blanket over her legs. Gold morning light was rimming the mountains, softening the edge of navy.

"You wanna hit a buffet this morning?" Elise asked. "The one in Planet Hollywood's in a basement. No windows. We can hang out a while."

Anthony lifted his eyebrows at her. "You don't eat."

"Buffets have coffee."

"Are you feeling sick? Can demons get sick?" He reached over to check her temperature, and Elise knocked his hand aside.

"I just don't want to sleep yet," she said.

The desert was waking up. Lizards rustled in the bush.

"All right, buffet sounds good. But you better hurry," Anthony said. "I'll grab McIntyre and the ladies? Bring them along?"

She grimaced. "The ladies" meant Tish McIntyre and their two preschool aged children, who were as domesticated as daimarachnids. Taking those little beasts into public was asking for trouble. "You're kidding, right?"

"Elise Kavanagh wants to hang out all morning at a buffet. That's crazy. I'm just testing how crazy you are. Should I bring 'em?"

She tucked the knife in her boot. She dropped the whetstone into her waist bag. "Sure, if the girls are awake." They would be awake. McIntyre's little ones, Deb and Dana, were usually an hour into their morning cartoons by the time the sun rose.

"Crazy," Anthony muttered. But he was smiling.

Elise didn't feel crazy. She just felt...content. "I'll see you there." She tossed the reflective blanket back at him, tilted her face to the shadows fleeing the sky, and willed herself away.